Out of the Fog

OUT OF THE FOG

CLARISSA ROSS

Thorndike Press • Chivers Press
Waterville, Maine USA   Bath, England

This Large Print edition is published by Thorndike Press, USA and by Chivers Press, England.

Published in 2002 in the U.S. by arrangement with Maureen Moran Agency.

Published in 2002 in the U.K. by arrangement with the author.

U.S. Hardcover 0-7862-4037-7 (Romance Series)
U.K. Hardcover 0-7540-4859-4 (Chivers Large Print)
U.K. Softcover 0-7540-4860-8 (Camden Large Print)

The text of this Large Print edition is unabridged.
Other aspects of the book may vary from the original edition.

Set in 16 pt. Plantin by Al Chase.

Printed in the United States on permanent paper.

British Library Cataloguing-in-Publication Data available

Library of Congress Cataloging-in-Publication Data

Ross, Clarissa, 1912–
Out of the fog / Clarissa Ross.
p. cm.
ISBN 0-7862-4037-7 (lg. print : hc : alk. paper)
1. Maine — Fiction. 2. Private investigators — Maine — Fiction. 3. Large type books. I. Title.
PR9199.3.R5996 O89 2002
813′.54—dc21 2001058277

To Alice Sachs, editor and friend

CHAPTER ONE

Spring comes as a drawn-out, gray, miserable period in Maine. When, farther south, green grass and buds on the trees are already appearing, Maine has nothing but the dried-up, colorless remnants of vegetation that have withstood winter's assaults. And the warming air comes to battle with the cold of the ocean and the hidden pockets of snow in the depths of thick woods to cause an onslaught of misty days and nights.

For weeks at a time the bleak Maine coast is plagued by fog with sunny days in the minority. And it was those days of ghostly fog that Vera Waters would always remember when she recalled the terror she had known that certain spring in the ancient Tudor-style house in a suburb of Portland. For they had come to her out of the ghostly mist, that group of people, who were to play such an ominous role in her affairs.

And as she remembered them they seemed now more like ghosts than people who had ever really lived. Sorry phantom figures linked together in eerie tragedy and drawn to her because she reminded them of a horror that could not be erased from their minds. A horror which was in danger of being repeated because she innocently was the bait for a tormented insane killer!

One day she would return to Portland and that English-style gabled house in the suburbs. She would stand in its dark living room and stare out the too small windows at the imposing Colonial house adjacent and remember what had gone on there. But she would not return in spring with its gray, foggy days. She would go when the area was in the full bloom of summer or perhaps when the quaint house with its particular vergeboard edging under its gables was mantled with winter snow. Anytime but in the spring.

When her arthritic-ridden Aunt Samantha had invited her to go to Portland and be her companion-nurse it had seemed a fine opportunity. Aunt Samantha Waters was the childless widow of her father's older brother and had been left wealthy in both investments and property. In inviting Vera to live with her, she had made it clear that her reward would be inheritance of the estate. Vera would have willingly joined the old woman without that special inducement since at the time the offer came she had been lonely and discouraged with her life in Boston.

She'd trained to be a librarian and readily found a position with one of the leading Boston museums. In the beginning she'd enjoyed her work but soon found she had a domineering female in authority over her. A woman who seemed to take a pleasure in proving her inefficient whenever possible. Vera had put up with this unhappy situation because she'd formed a romantic attachment for a young man associated with another branch of the museum's work.

But the young man had suddenly been transferred to a different city and the romance had come to nothing. Vera was living alone in a small apartment on Beacon Hill as her parents had moved to a Florida community on her father's retirement. Faced with the prospect of finding another job or carrying on in the one which was making her unhappy, she accepted her Aunt Samantha's offer as an ideal way out of her dilemma.

It hadn't taken long to sublet her furnished apartment and wind up her affairs in Boston. Because Aunt Samantha had previously shown little interest in her or the other members of the family, she'd never met the old woman although there were fewer than a hundred miles between Boston and Portland. Before definitely agreeing to join her aunt, Vera had talked to her father on a long distance phone call.

From his sunny Florida sanctuary her father had cheerfully advised her to move to Portland. "No reason why you should hesitate," her father said. "In the old days your mother and I used to see a lot of Samantha and my brother. Then there was the misunderstanding about your grandfather's estate and ill feelings developed. I always felt I had been treated badly. So we stopped seeing each other. If, in her final days, Samantha wants to repair the wrong and be fair with you, why not let her?"

"Why not?" Vera had said with a small rueful laugh. "Her letter sounded very businesslike and stiff. What sort of person is she?"

"Regal might be a good word to describe her," her father had said. "She's from one of the famous New Bedford whaling families. Long line of bluebloods. She's tall and thin and no beauty. But she has that stern New England type of features that have a fine quality of their own."

"She sounds formidable."

"Unless she's changed, she can be," her father agreed. "But Samantha always had character. I wouldn't worry about her being difficult to live with. It could be a helpful experience for you."

"I hope so," she'd said. "I don't think she's in good health. In her letter she speaks of arthritis."

"A family disease with her people as I recall it," her father said. "Too bad it should strike Samantha. There is one other thing I remember about her. She's extremely interested in spiritualism."

"Oh?" Vera wasn't certain this was pleasant news.

"Typical of her to approach it in a very practical way," her father said. "She's not the type to create a spooky atmosphere around her. But she does live in a fascinating old house that is said to be haunted. And she enjoys trying to commune with the spirits departed. At least she did years ago. She may have lost interest in that by now."

"I hope so."

"Don't let it worry you," her father had advised. "Your mother and I plan to visit Maine this summer. If you decide to live with Samantha in Portland, we'll arrange to rent a cottage near there."

"That would be wonderful," she'd said, as she missed them.

And so she had at once gotten in touch

with Samantha Waters and told her she would accept her offer and join her in a few days. Vera drove her tiny sedan to the large Maine coastal city. Fortunately, it happened to be one of the few bright, sunny days of that particular spring. She found the fine old English-style Tudor house on a dead-end street of the suburbs. There were three other homes on this elm-shaded street, though the elms were still leafless in March, and she later learned that Aunt Samantha owned them all. At the time of her arrival, a large white Colonial adjoining her aunt's place was empty as was a small cottage on the opposite side of the street.

At that moment these things meant nothing to her. Later they were to play a prominent part in the macabre turn of events in which she became involved. Her Aunt Samantha turned out to be the no-nonsense type that Vera's father had described. The old woman received her for the first time in the huge, shadowed living room. All the rooms in the ancient house were too dark because the pseudo-English windows were dismally small and there weren't enough of them. But the mansion was elegant with fine wood-paneling and luxurious, antique furniture which loomed richly in the gloom.

Aunt Samantha sat in a wheelchair and studied Vera with steely eyes set under heavy, gray eyebrows. Arthritis had bent her back and she was so thin, she appeared emaciated. Yet her hollow-cheeked, leathery old face had a proud air of defiance about it. Her features were aristocratic and her manner was sharp.

"I'm not obliged to remain in this wheelchair," she informed Vera at once. "I can walk a little. But I prefer the chair most of the time because walking is painful for me. I have an elevator chair installed on the stairway and another wheelchair at the landing on the second floor. So I have good mobility on the two floors."

Seated on the divan opposite the old woman and aware she was under skeptical appraisal, Vera ventured, "That sounds well arranged."

"I pride myself on running my household affairs in an orderly fashion!" The old woman delivered this with a sniff.

Vera glanced around her in the blue-shadowed atmosphere. "It is such a large house."

"I have a housekeeper, a cook, and a general maid plus a handy man," Aunt Samantha said. "Help like that costs a fortune and are hard to keep these days but I manage very well."

"I'm sure that you do," she said.

The craggy face was frowning. "You look like a sensible young woman," her aunt was saying. "You have the long blond hair and blue eyes of your mother and even Waters features of your father. I'm glad you wear your hair shoulder length. I despise short hair."

"I've never considered changing it."

"Don't," the old woman said crisply. "You are a pretty girl in a studious sort of way. I like that. I think a serious face is better than a pretty vacant one. And I'm glad you don't wear glasses."

"I sometimes do when I read."

"Don't," Aunt Samantha snapped. It seemed a favorite word with her. Her clawlike hands clutched the arms of her wheelchair. "I wore them when I was your age and lost a good match that way. I was an old maid before I had another chance and married your uncle. But by that time I'd learned enough to shun glasses. They may suit some faces but not mine or yours."

"I've never given it any thought," Vera smiled.

"It's wise to think about everything," the old woman in the wheelchair warned her.

"I've always carefully planned my life and every move I've made. I thought a good deal before I got in touch with you. I wasn't sure your father would allow you to come here."

"He thinks it's a good idea as long as I'm willing."

Aunt Samantha grimaced. "That's pleasant news. For too long a time we've kept apart. The family is dwindling. There is no one on my side. And it is right the feud between us should end and you be here."

"I'm sure I'll like it," she ventured hopefully though she was beginning already to wonder if it mightn't be too quiet and isolated a way of life for her to endure.

Her aunt seemed to read her thoughts for she said, "I have no intention of making you the kind of prisoner I am in this big house. You'll have the opportunity of finding new friends here and leading an active social life. In the summer there is golf and boating."

She smiled. "It sounds good. Boston is so hot in summer."

The eaglelike eyes peered at her through the shadows. "Are you engaged or anything of that sort?"

"No," she said. "There was someone but it's over now."

"I won't ask questions," the old woman said primly. "I'm glad you won't be pining for someone in Boston or somewhere else. You'll find lots of nice young men here to occupy you."

"That doesn't worry me."

"It should," Aunt Samantha snapped. "How old are you? Twenty-one? Twenty?"

"Twenty-two." She was glad of the gloom because she was blushing.

"You see," the old woman said. "It's time you were finding someone. I know from my own experience. You'll be meeting John Murchison, my lawyer, he's very pleasant and I'll have him introduce you to his circle."

"There's no necessity for that," she protested.

"Don't forget I plan everything carefully," the woman in the wheelchair reminded her. "I hope you're not devoted to television. I consider it an idiot's delight and don't have a set in the house."

She smiled wanly. "I'm not an addict. I can manage without it."

"You should be able to if you have normal intelligence," Aunt Samantha said with asperity. "You'll find radios all over the house and a stereo in the back parlor. I like good music. I'm also interested in spiritualism."

"My father made some mention of that."

The old woman scowled. "I imagine he

didn't approve. I don't recall him as being a believer."

"He didn't offer any opinion," Vera said quickly. "He just spoke of it in passing."

"I see," Aunt Samantha said dubiously. "Well, I derive a great deal of comfort from it."

"I'm glad."

"That is a Ouija board over there," the old woman nodded to a small table on her left. "I have several. I believe that I'm able to get messages from the other world using them."

"I know nothing about it."

"Your tone of voice tells me you don't believe. But perhaps I can win you over. You may find it hard to accept that I discussed your coming here with the spirit of my late husband. And on that very board he spelled out the letters to give me word of approval."

Vera felt a tiny chill go through her as her eyes fixed on the apparatus with its indicator, a triangular piece of wood which could be moved under the finger tips of one or more persons to spell out words from the alphabet printed on the board. So her dead uncle had welcomed her by means of a message there!

In a small voice she asked the old woman, "Do you consult the Ouija board a good deal?"

"Constantly," Samantha said. "I believe I have certain powers of a medium. I could probably have been a professional if I'd wished. But I'm content to have it as a hobby."

"I see."

"It has been invaluable to me," the woman in the wheelchair said. "As important in my dealing with the living as in my relationships with the dead. Something does survive us you know."

The shadows in the gloomy room seemed to close in on them more so that she could barely see the hawk face of the old woman seated opposite her. She said, "I'm afraid I'm too young to have given it much thought."

"Age has nothing to do with it. One of the spirits I communicate with regularly died as a girl of twelve."

Again she experienced an icy hand on her spine at this casual reference to contact with the dead. "People do die at all ages," she agreed.

"The spirit is what is important," Aunt Samantha said with intensity. "That is what remains active on the other side. They direct us even when we aren't aware of it."

"You really feel that?"

"I know it," the old woman said firmly. "But there will be plenty of time for you to learn about such things. Now I want you to make yourself comfortable here. I'll have the housekeeper show you to your room. And believe me when I say that I have brought you here for your good as well as mine."

"Thank you," she said in reply to this rather odd speech of welcome. And she rose to be escorted upstairs by the housekeeper.

Mrs. Gaskell, the middle-aged woman who ran the household for her aunt, was a quiet, rather sour woman. She had a pasty face and eyes that continually hinted of disapproval. And she made Vera nervous.

The room on the second floor rear to which Vera found herself assigned was large enough and had its own bathroom. But there was something cold and forbidding about it which she found characteristic of the entire house.

Mrs. Gaskell switched on the ceiling light to show the room's ivory and blue decor in drapes and wallpaper with matching bedspread. "The daylight is not good anywhere in the house," she warned her. "On dull days we have to use electric lights in every room."

"It's a shame the windows are so small," Vera said.

"Builder wanted to out-do the English I guess," the housekeeper said glumly. "It's not to my taste. If there's anything you need let me know."

The housekeeper left her alone to unpack. With a sigh Vera glanced around the room again before settling in. It was large, neat and pleasantly appointed and yet it had a kind of cold, brooding atmosphere which she could not understand. She went to the window and saw there was a small garden area directly below which looked colorless and bleak in the early spring season. In the middle of it was a concrete fountain or perhaps a large bird bath not in use. And to the left she could see the rear of the large Colonial house which seemed to be unoccupied.

She left the window to begin unpacking her bags and hanging up her things in the ample closet attached to the room. She was still doing this when she heard a creaking sound from the hallway and then Aunt Samantha propelled herself into the room in a wheelchair.

The old woman gave her a grim smile. "You needn't be surprised. I told you I have a chair on every floor and my stair elevator to convey me up and down to them."

She paused in her work. "I'd forgotten."

Samantha glanced around the room. "Do you like it?"

"Yes."

The sharp old eyes fixed on her. "You don't feel anything strange about it?"

Vera hesitated. Dare she be honest and admit the room seemed cold in a weird way she couldn't explain. She compromised, telling the woman in the wheelchair, "I don't know exactly how to answer you."

A crafty smile crossed the ancient crone's leathery face. She leaned forward in the chair. "It makes you a little uneasy?"

"Perhaps. But I don't understand why. It's a very nice room."

Aunt Samantha chuckled. "Your answer pleases me."

She stared at her. "It does?"

"Yes. I purposely picked this room for you because of a theory I had. I received an impression concerning you as soon as we met."

"Oh?"

The old woman's bright eyes held her. "I believe you share some of my psychic powers. I can sense that in others."

"I'm sure you're wrong," she protested.

"No!" The old woman raised one of her thin hands to dismiss any argument. "I can't be deceived on such matters. With just some training you could be in touch with the spirit world as I am. What you've said about this room proves it. And it is why I had Mrs. Gaskell put you in here."

Alarm took hold of her. In a taut voice, she asked, "You're saying there is something special about this room?"

"You've already said it."

"But not anything I can properly explain," she said, upset. "Please tell me what you mean."

The old woman in the wheelchair smiled derisively. "Years ago a girl who lived in this house and occupied this very room met a violent death. She had an unfortunate love affair with the owner of the house next door. He had a jealous wife who wouldn't give him his freedom. So he and the girl made a suicide pact. They met in the house next door one night when the wife was away. The man shot her and then himself."

"How awful!" Vera gasped, shocked by the account. And with a feeling of horror she realized that one of her first moves after coming to the room had been to go to the window and stare at the house next door. She had seemed impelled to do so.

"You can see the window of the suicide room from the window here," Aunt

Samantha went on in her elderly, rasping tone.

"Was this very long ago?" Vera asked.

"A half century," her aunt said. "But the house next door has had the reputation of ill-luck and being haunted ever since. During the time I've owned it there's been more than one tragedy of sudden death, accident or fatal illness associated with it. As a result of the bad name given it, I can't seem to rent it for any lengthy period. It's empty now."

"I noticed that," she said. "And so is the cottage across the street."

"The cottage is another matter," the older woman said. "I have no trouble getting tenants for it. But I ask a high rental and that there be no children. So often, as happens right now, it is vacant for a little while."

She managed a bleak smile. "At least it isn't haunted."

"Does the story bother you?"

She shrugged. "I find it unpleasant."

Aunt Samantha eyed her sharply. "No one has ever complained of seeing a ghost in here. But if you'd rather be moved I'll speak to Mrs. Gaskell."

Again Vera hesitated. She would have much preferred to have been transferred to some other room but she had a shrewd idea this would annoy her aunt. The old woman felt one should betray no dread of the spirit world and to show fear of the odd atmosphere of this room would surely displease her. And she wanted to make a favorable impression.

So she said, "I'm willing to stay here."

"You're sure?"

"Yes."

"I say you're wise," the old woman in the wheelchair said. "No harm will come to you and you may gain much more than you realize from the experience."

With this strange statement the old woman propelled herself back into the shadowed hallway and vanished. Somewhat shaken by the conversation Vera resumed her unpacking. She's never believed in ghosts and she wasn't going to allow herself to be panicked by this story. But it had made an uncomfortable impression on her. One she would have to fight.

Dinner proved to be a much more pleasant event than Vera could have hoped. When she had dressed and gone downstairs she found her aunt in the living room with a handsome, brown-haired young man in black tie and dinner jacket. He had a bronzed, friendly face that lighted with pleasure as she entered the room.

From her wheelchair, Aunt Samantha said, "My niece, Vera Waters, this is my lawyer, John Murchison. I wanted you two to meet as quickly as possible so dinner tonight seemed ideal."

The young man advanced to Vera with an outstretched hand. "I've looked forward to this," he told her.

She smiled. "My aunt has spoken to me about you."

His handshake was firm and meaningful. And the old woman in the wheelchair at once spoke up indicating that John Murchison was regarded more as one of the family than the family lawyer. That there was to be no formality between them and that she very much wanted them to be close friends. It was in this mood that they moved on into the dining room.

Vera found the house had much more feeling of warmth and hospitality at night. It lent itself to artificial lighting. The bleakness of the sparse light from the too-tiny windows no longer was an annoyance after dark. And as they sat at the richly appointed table she forgot some of her unhappy feelings about the mansion.

During the course of dinner she learned that John Murchison was a bachelor who devoted little of his time to legal affairs but most of his attention was given to a real estate business he had carefully built up. It was in this capacity he acted mostly for her aunt. He also enjoyed golf and had a powerboat of medium size. By the time the meal was over she felt she knew the pleasant young man very well.

They returned to the living room for coffee and after-dinner drinks and then Aunt Samantha abruptly announced her intention of retiring for the night. "But no need for you young people to end your evening together," she insisted. "In fact I want John to take this opportunity of telling you more about my plans."

So they saw her to the stair elevator and said their goodnights. Then, a trifle embarrassed, Vera returned to the living room with the young lawyer. He led her to a divan by a large black marble fireplace and when she had seated herself he stood before her.

"I guess your aunt wants me to tell you about her will," he said.

She smiled uneasily. "That's so silly. I've only just gotten here. It's not all that interesting to me."

"Still I should carry out her wishes."

She shrugged. "If you think you must."

"Everything is to go to you on her death," he said. And then as if she mightn't have understood, he added, "Everything."

"The money isn't what brought me here."

"You'll be a rich young woman," John Murchison promised her.

"I hope Aunt Samantha lives a very long time."

He smiled. "In spite of her arthritis I'd say there is a good chance that she will. And even when she does die you may not be done with her. You know of her interest in spiritualism?"

"Yes. I don't share it though."

"Still she may try to reach you from the other side when the time comes," he suggested.

Vera gave a tiny shiver. "I find it a grisly thought."

"She doesn't. She's very earthy about her spiritual leanings." And they both laughed at this small joke of his.

The young man studied her earnestly. "I hope you find it pleasant here. Before you came your aunt had another will. In it her money was left mostly to a local charity and her servants. In the new document the local charity is left out and the servants given a nominal but I feel fair bequest. I mention this because it is possible some of the household staff may resent you for that reason."

Vera frowned. "I didn't know. But it did

seem to me that Mrs. Gaskell wasn't overfriendly."

He gave her an understanding nod. "That's not a surprise. Mrs. Gaskell voiced her annoyance about the changed will to me. I can't see why your aunt chose to tell the servants about it. But then she's not a woman who's always easy to understand."

She sighed. "Perhaps I shouldn't have come here at all."

"I wouldn't feel that way," he said. And with another of his warm smiles, he went on, "Speaking for myself I'm glad you did. Your aunt wants me to take you under my wing and introduce you socially in the city."

Vera smiled wanly. "You mustn't feel any obligation. I'll make my own friends."

"Why not let me begin by being the first one?"

She blushed. "I'd find that pleasant."

"One other thing," he told her. "Beginning at once you will be acting for your aunt in matters of real estate."

This did come as a surprise. Her eyes widened. "But I have no experience!"

"Your aunt wants you to gain it while she's still alive to advise you if necessary," he said. "That's the whole idea."

"She didn't mention this."

"It was left to me," John assured her. "So

we'll be working together very closely in the matter of rentals. And they form an important part of the estate's income."

She sighed. "You'll have to explain it all to me."

John showed pleasure at the idea. "I'll enjoy it," he said. "And I have some immediate good news to prove you may be just what we needed to change our luck. I have some people interested in renting the Colonial house next door. They'll be coming tomorrow to take a look at it, so you'll be meeting them. And that house has been almost impossible to rent."

Vera gave him a meaningful look as she said quietly, "You're talking about the haunted house."

He looked slightly surprised. "You know about it?"

"Aunt Samantha told me. It's a strange story. When these people find out, do you think they'll still want the house?"

John Murchison hesitated. "That's the odd part of it. In this case it was their hearing about the legend of the house being haunted that brought the prospective tenants to me. They're interested in a haunted house!"

CHAPTER TWO

Vera was startled. "I find that very unusual," she said.

He spread his hands. "We run across all kinds of odd customers in the real estate business," he told her. "This family happens to have an interest in the supernatural. At least one of the group does. It's two brothers and the wife of the younger brother is the party who wrote me. She made it plain she'd heard about the house and was interested in an old house with a history."

"Even one with a dark history?"

"Apparently so," John Murchison said. "They have been living in Boston but are anxious to get away to a smaller city. So they'll be here tomorrow to look at the house. I'll bring them over to meet you afterwards."

She was dismayed at the prospect. "If it's to talk business I won't know what to say!"

The young man standing before her laughed. "Don't let it worry you. Leave it all to me. From what I've been able to learn these people are very wealthy. Their family name is Harper. Ever hear of them?"

"No."

"I understand they are a branch of an old Boston family. It would seem neither of the brothers has business interests to keep them in the city so they are probably living on income. They ought to like it here."

"Is the Colonial house furnished?"

"They asked me about that," the young lawyer said. "It is. But they probably would want to get rid of a lot of the stuff and bring in their own things. Both the Colonial house and the cottage are furnished and we have been renting them that way."

"Does Aunt Samantha know about these people coming?"

"Yes. She's especially interested because the woman is an adherent of spiritualism. But she wants you to interview them as part of your new responsibilities."

Vera grimaced. "I'm apt to be a disappointment to her."

"I don't believe that," John Murchison said. "You'll soon get the knack of things. I can understand that just arriving here it all seems very strange to you."

"That's too true."

He smiled. "Your aunt is not an unkind woman. As you get to know her better you'll find that out. And you'll become accustomed to her eccentricities."

She gave him a rueful look. "The spiritualism thing bothers me most." And she turned to glance at the Ouija board on its table. Then she asked, "Does she really believe the dead communicate to her through that?"

"Yes."

Vera sighed. "I find that a little mad."

"Because it's new to you," he suggested. "The Ouija board is one of the means used by spiritualists to contact those on the other side. It is widely accepted."

"Not by me," she said, rising.

"Nor by me," he said agreeably. "But I don't try to impose my beliefs on others. If your aunt gets some comfort from it, I consider it a relatively harmless pastime."

She gave a tiny shudder. "I think of it as creepy and unhealthful. And I think her interest in that haunted house next door is equally unpleasant."

"That long ago suicide and murder has the kind of romantic aura to it that makes such legends live," the young lawyer said. "Your aunt has carefully collected information concerning the tragic affair. Have you seen the picture of the woman in the case? The one who lived here."

"No," she said, feeling just a small sense

of panic. "But I believe I'm in what was her bedroom."

"Interesting," he said. "I'll show you her photo. It's one of those large, old-fashioned oval enlargements." And he guided her across the living room to a wall liberally covered with framed paintings and photographs of various styles and sizes. He halted before a large one with an ornate gilt frame. Its gray oval depths showed the sad, yet lovely face of a young woman in high collar dress of the era and upswept hairdo. "There she is," he commented.

"She's a beauty!" Vera gasped.

"Obviously that beauty brought both her and the man to their deaths," he said. "I'd imagine it's only rarely that an ugly woman brings about a suicide pact between lovers."

She stared at the sad face and the large tragic eyes of the woman in the photograph for a few seconds longer, then forced herself to turn away from its morbid fascination. With a frown, she asked him, "Do you think it right for my aunt to keep that hung here?"

He shrugged. "It makes a good conversation piece and she also seems to feel it helps her materialize the departed spirit of the woman."

Vera's eyebrows lifted. "She believes she

has actually talked to her?"

"Many times," he said with a faint smile. "You'll hear about it from her, I'm sure."

"I won't encourage her to discuss it," she promised.

They talked for a little longer and then he left with a promise to bring the three people interested in the Colonial house over to meet her around the middle of the following afternoon. She saw him to the door and when he took her hand for a final handshake he held it in a warm grip just long enough to let her know that he had, at the least, a friendly interest in her. She closed the door after him feeling that she was lucky to have someone like him to guide her through the first puzzling days in this strange and unusual atmosphere.

Her sleep that night was restless and troubled by nightmares. John Murchison had kindled her imagination in showing her the photograph of the murdered beauty. And it was a natural consequence that her dreams should be haunted by the sad face. In vivid fashion she conjured a fantasy of the tragic figure standing by her bedside. Then she watched as the lovely creature crossed to the window and looked out toward the house next door. Perhaps watching for some signal from her lover.

It was so frighteningly real that in the small hours of the morning Vera rose up in bed with a startled cry as she tried to fend off the murdered beauty. She awoke from her nightmare in a state of cold perspiration and trembling. When she realized it had been a bad dream she forced herself to lie back on her pillow. But for a long while before sleep made her eyelids droop shut again she stared up into the murky shadows of the room with fear in her eyes.

She awakened in the morning to gray daylight and the distant monotonous chant of a foghorn. Getting out of bed she went to the window to discover that the sunshine of the day before had vanished to leave the area wreathed in a phantom cloak of thick gray mist. With a sigh she turned away from the dismal view and began readying herself for the day ahead.

Breakfast was a solitary affair served by a dour, middle-aged maid. As Vera was having her coffee Mrs. Gaskell came into the dining room briefly to inform her, "Mrs. Waters never comes down to breakfast. You'll not likely see her until near noon."

She offered her thanks for this information and asked if it was usual for it to be as foggy as it was. "Such a thick fog!" she exclaimed.

"More foggy days than fine ones at this

season," was the housekeeper's grim prediction and she swept out of the room to other pursuits.

Vera filled in some of the morning learning the geography of the mansion. It was divided into three wings and none of the rooms was especially large except the living room. She decided her favorite room on the lower floor was the rear parlor where the large, expensive stereo set ran almost the length of one wall. She examined the records stored in the record compartment of the set and found many of the classics that were favorites of hers. She had a liking for symphony groups and selecting a promising recording of the *Peer Gynt Suite* sat down in an easy chair of the room to listen to it. She soon lost herself in the majesty of the music as she sat there in the shadows.

The selection was still playing when her Aunt Samantha appeared in the doorway of the room in her wheelchair. The hawklike face of the old woman showed approval and she nodded to her without making any effort at conversation until the music ended. Then the old woman propelled herself into the center of the room.

The alert, sunken eyes regarded her with interest. "You like good music?"

"Yes."

"At least that's one thing we share," her aunt said. "Did you rest well last night?"

Vera hesitated. "For the most part," she finally said.

Aunt Samantha crooked an eyebrow. "What sort of answer is that?"

She made a futile gesture with her right hand. "I seemed to dream a lot."

"Oh?" Those sharp eyes were glued on her. "What sort of dreams?"

She felt embarrassment. "Put it down to nerves and getting used to a strange room," she said.

"What did you dream about?"

Vera swallowed hard. "Mostly about that woman who was murdered. I thought I saw her in the room. John Murchison showed me her photograph in the living room last night. I'm afraid I let it impress me too much."

To her surprise her aunt's reaction was one of grim amusement rather than annoyance. "Your dreams don't astonish me," she said. "Remember I told you that I believe you're psychic."

"I don't think that's the explanation," she said.

"You will see," her aunt promised. In the distance the foghorn gave another of its monotonous blasts. The old woman frowned. "We would have one of these awful days when those people are coming to look at the house."

"John Murchison spoke of them."

"Did he tell you I expected you to interview them?"

Vera gave the old woman an imploring look. "I don't think I'm ready for that sort of thing."

"You have to begin some time. Why not now?"

Grasping at any straw, she said, "But if this Harper woman is a devotee of spiritualism, I'd imagine you'd want to talk to her yourself. You probably would have a lot to discuss."

"That can wait," the old woman said dryly. "I'm not one to tell every stranger of my beliefs until I get to know them well. So many of them are charlatans and others just plain silly!"

"I hadn't thought of that," she admitted.

"You will by the time you've lived as long as I," Aunt Samantha promised darkly. And then with startling abruptness she asked, "Do you have a second given name I'm not familiar with?"

"My full name is Anne Vera," she said, not understanding what was in the old woman's mind.

The emaciated face showed thoughtfulness. "Do you have a close friend named

Jane or maybe June? Anyone living or dead?"

She considered a moment. "No," she said at last. "I have no friend by that name. Why?"

"Last night the Ouija board spelled out the name of June and then Jane for me," Aunt Samantha declared. "I know it was meant to be a message of some kind. Perhaps a warning. I wondered if it had to do with you."

"I'm sure it hasn't."

"Don't be too sure," the rasping voice warned her. "I have the feeling that it has whether you know it or not."

Vera didn't like being involved in this kind of conversation. She stared at the old woman in the murky light of the quiet room and thought what a weird figure she was. And how filled with fantastic beliefs of the spirit world.

Wanting to change the subject, she said, "What will I say to the Harpers when they come?"

"Be pleasant with them and leave all the business details to John."

"Do you want to rent to them?"

"If John is satisfied I'm sure I'll approve," Aunt Samantha said. "He is a very smart young man. But you've probably noticed that without my telling you."

"He seems very nice."

"He is very nice," the old woman snapped. "Just the sort of young man I'd set my cap for if I were your age."

Once again Vera found her aunt's outspokenness embarrassing. She said, "I hardly know him yet."

"You'll be seeing a lot of him from now on," her aunt predicted. "We'll just hope the fog lifts this afternoon and makes the area look more inviting for those people from Boston."

But the fog didn't lift. If anything it became thicker as the afternoon progressed. When luncheon was over Aunt Samantha took the chair elevator upstairs again and did not reappear. Vera knew the old woman was deliberately absenting herself so she would have to conduct the interview with the Harpers on her own.

She became impatient and found herself standing by the window of the reception hall watching for John Murchison to appear with the prospective tenants of the Colonial house. It wasn't until a few minutes after three that she saw a car roll up out of the fog and park before the empty house. A moment later John stepped out of the car to hold the door open for the others. She watched as they emerged in the thick mist to stand with him glancing up at the Colonial house in an appraising manner. In the murky fog the newcomers seemed to have a slim sameness about them — black, spare figures ascending the stairs in the gray mist.

They went inside and she began to have a feeling of suspense concerning them. What would their impression of the old house be? She could picture the young lawyer moving briskly from one dark and deserted room to another, pointing out the strong points of the bleak haunted mansion as the white dust covers of the furniture formed a company of sullen, phantom witnesses.

She frowned slightly as she stood there alone gazing at the fog-shrouded Colonial house. What sort of people would deliberately seek out a house with its dark history? And the face of the lovely lost lady whose bedroom she now occupied and who had haunted her dreams last night came to her mind's eye again. And to her astonishment she almost felt a resentment toward the company who were at this moment exploring the house of suicide and murder.

As if she were identifying with the long dead beauty in her thoughts! This made her turn from the window and move slowly in the direction of the living room with concern marring her own attractive blondness. Was her Aunt Samantha more perceptive than she believed? Was she actually sensitive to the psychic to a greater degree than she'd ever guessed?

She was still standing in the living room pondering on this when the doorbell rang. Mrs. Gaskell quickly appeared to open the door and show John Murchison and the strangers in. She stood there bracing herself against her nervousness as the young lawyer in a dark raincoat came toward her smiling.

"The Harpers have been looking forward to meeting you," he said. And turning, he indicated a rather handsome middle-aged couple smartly dressed in wet weather wear. There was an older man standing behind them but Vera couldn't get a good look at him.

The younger of the men who had a matinee idol's classic even features marred only by a hint of weakness came forward with a smile. He was dark of hair and eyes with an olive tinge to his skin. "I'm James Harper," he told her, as he shook hands. Then turning, he added, "And this is my wife, Maria."

Maria smiled thinly. "How do you do, Miss Waters." She was also dark and thin with the appearance of a person plagued by a frail constitution. There were dark circles under her eyes to mar an otherwise pleasant face and the eyes were sad and haunted. It was easy to believe that she might be a person drawn to the cult of spiritualism.

"And this is my brother, William," James Harper went on. As he spoke the older man moved forward to confront Vera. He was a very different type from his brother and seemed by his graying hair and lined face to be at least ten years older than James Harper, yet she doubted that he was. His face was more angular than handsome and there was a look of ruthless strength in the keen black eyes, the thin-bridged nose and the narrow face with its bluish beard line. He had the kind of heavy beard whose shadow no amount of close shaving could erase.

"We understand you are also a newcomer to Portland, Miss Waters," he said studying her with a strange intensity.

"I am," she agreed. And because his searching gaze made her uncomfortable, she let her eyes wander to the others. But this gave her no respite for she was shocked to discover that they were staring at her in the same odd fashion.

"We find the house Mr. Murchison showed us rather large for us, though it is interesting," William Harper said with those sharp black eyes still boring through her.

She offered him a faltering smile. "I'm sure Mr. Murchison pointed out its many advantages."

The handsome James Harper stepped up by his brother again. "I'd say Mr. Murchison did an excellent job," he assured her.

John gave her a meaningful glance. "I explained to these good people that the grounds and even the building would be much more appealing on a more pleasant day."

"That is true," she agreed, taking this cue from him. She managed an uneasy smile for the strangers. "Surely you'd like some hot coffee or a drink of some kind?"

"I would enjoy a cup of hot coffee," the sad-eyed Maria Harper said. "And I'm certain my husband and his brother would also."

"Fine," Vera said. "I'll speak to Mrs. Gaskell."

She left the living room for a moment, relieved to be free of their staring eyes. Why did they look at her in that odd manner? It was almost rude on their part. Baffled and uneasy she went to the kitchen and gave her request for coffee to a sullen Mrs. Gaskell who promised to relay it to the cook. Vera then made the return trip along the dark hallway to the living room wishing that her aunt would appear and take over her duties.

When she returned to the living room she found the others seated in a corner in a rough type of semicircle. The men rose as she entered and she quickly took a chair beside John Murchison.

William Harper was studying her intently again and with a probing expression on his thin face, he said, "Since you are a newcomer here you actually know little about the history of the house next door."

"Just what I've been told since my arrival," she said.

Maria Harper told her, "It was written up in *Down East Magazine* a year or two ago. They called it the most noted haunted house in Portland. And they gave a long account of the tragedy and the history of the house since. Some claim it brings its tenants bad luck."

John Murchison gave the frail woman a smile. "You aren't that superstitious, I'm sure."

The too handsome, almost feminine, face of James Harper showed a smile in return. "I can promise you such a story would only prove a challenge to my wife. She is very much interested in investigating the supernatural. I'm afraid my brother and I have less enthusiasm for it."

"None at all," was William Harper's dry comment.

The frail Maria looked sadly amused. "You see, Miss Waters, I alone of the three of us possess a questioning mind."

"I find that interesting," Vera said, again conscious that their eyes hardly left her. They seemed unaware of how much attention they were giving her. She wondered if this behavior was usual with them and if they knew how nervous they were making her feel.

"It is a charming area," James Harper said. "I can tell that even on this miserable day. And this quiet dead-end street offers great privacy."

"No question of that," John Murchison said.

"We would not consider a long lease until we had given the house a trial," William Harper said.

"I think those matters could be easily arranged," the young lawyer assured them.

The weakly handsome face of James Harper mirrored his keen interest in her as he said, "We would be neighbors, Miss Waters. And since we are all new to the area we could learn about it together."

"That's true," she said without much enthusiasm. Their staring was making her uneasy and she wished the coffee would be served and they would go.

After what seemed a long delay the maid arrived with a tray bearing coffee and some cookies. Vera rather shakily presided over the coffee cups conscious that she was still the center of attention and not knowing why. John Murchison apparently sensed her nervousness and kept the conversation going with talk of the history of Portland. She was grateful to him for this.

Finally the Harpers rose to leave. And she saw them to the door without their giving any clear indication of whether they would rent the house or not. The last to leave was William Harper and he lingered on the steps in the fog a moment after the others had moved on toward the car.

"I've been most impressed meeting you, Miss Waters," he said, his thin face showing a look of sincerity.

"Thank you," she said, wondering why she should mean so much to him and thinking that this was merely small talk on his part.

"Whether we take the house or not I may come by again one day," the older of the Harper brothers suggested. "I'd like to learn more about the area and talk to you."

Thinking there was something distinctly odd in this as well as their undisguised staring at her she managed an awkward, "Well, then I'll likely be hearing from you later."

"Indeed you shall," he promised gravely with a last searching look at her. Then he nodded and went on down the steps to join the others.

She watched the car turn and vanish in the fog. Then she closed the door. It had been a strange experience and the Harper family had turned out to be very weird people. At least that was the way she felt about them on the basis of their talk and their staring at her.

A whirring sound caught her attention and she glanced up to see her Aunt Samantha descending the stairs in her single chair elevator. She went over and when the old woman reached the hallway she was quick to assist her into the wheelchair that had been left there.

Once settled in the wheelchair Aunt Samantha gave her a questioning glance. "Well, what did you make of them?"

"I found them very odd."

The old woman frowned. "In what way?"

Vera shrugged. "Something in their manner. A certain furtiveness. And then they seemed to be staring at me in a rude fashion most of the time they were here."

"You're a strikingly pretty girl. What's odd about their staring?"

"It wasn't that kind of staring," Vera protested.

"Indeed?" Aunt Samantha said. "And exactly what variety of stare would you consider they subjected you to?"

She shook her head unhappily. "It's hard to put into words. I seemed to fascinate them in some unpleasant way. They couldn't seem to take their eyes from me. I felt they were doing it almost against their will and yet they continued to do it."

Aunt Samantha's lean, leathery face showed interest. "I must say you do have a lively imagination. And that goes along with the psychic."

"Ask John Murchison when you see him again," she said. "I'm sure he must have noticed what was going on. He may be able to explain it to you better."

"I have no doubt of that. You haven't made it clear at all. Did they say they would take the house or did they do nothing but stare?"

Vera felt her cheeks burn. She resented her aunt's acid tongue and again wondered whether she'd made a wrong move in coming to Portland no matter how rich the rewards. She said, "They didn't arrive at any definite decision while they were here. But I think they are at least considering renting."

"John will let us know," the old woman said. "He generally has a final talk with them at his office. If he has any success, he'll be phoning us."

"Are you very anxious to rent the house?" Vera asked, standing by her aunt's wheelchair in the near darkness of the hallway. It struck her that if her aunt was as wealthy as she was said to be, the rental couldn't be all that important to her.

From the gloom the old woman in the wheelchair said, "She likes it rented."

"She?"

"The ghost of course," Aunt Samantha said with some indignation. "She's spelled that out for me on the Ouija board more than once."

Vera heard this with disbelief. "You can't be serious!"

"And why shouldn't I be? Don't you think they have feelings?"

"It's too fantastic!"

"Not at all. She doesn't like being there in that deserted house. She's much happier when someone is there."

Vera could hardly think of anything to say in reply to this. Fortunately she was saved from making a comment by the phone in the hallway ringing. She answered it and it was John Murchison on the line.

Sounding in a happy mood, he announced, "Good news. They've taken the house on a year's lease. I'll drop by on my way home and tell you and Mrs. Waters all the details."

"Thanks for letting us know," she said. And when she put down the phone she joined a waiting Aunt Samantha to inform her, "He rented the house."

"Good," the old woman said with satisfaction.

"He's dropping by here on his way home to tell us the full story," she said.

The old woman nodded. "Then he may as well stay for dinner. I'll tell Mrs. Gaskell there'll be three." And she wheeled herself off down the dark hall to the kitchen.

Feeling vaguely uneasy about the whole business of the afternoon Vera went upstairs to freshen up before John arrived. She changed into another more suitable dress for the evening and by the time she went downstairs again John was at the door.

She and Aunt Samantha received him in the living room. He was jubilant about renting the house. "They didn't quibble about price at all," he said. "And if they like it they plan to renew for a longer lease."

"That's fine," Aunt Samantha said. And then giving Vera a glance, she told him, "There is one matter I'd like to settle. Vera claims they are rather weird people."

John Murchison looked surprised. "Why do you think that?" he directed the question to Vera.

She gave her aunt a look and then told him, "It seemed to me they were staring at me oddly all the time they were here."

At once he smiled. "Oh, that?"

Vera stared at him. "You find it amusing?"

"No," he hastened to tell her. "You're right. They were staring at you. I wondered at the time. But later they explained to me. At least William Harper, the older brother, did. It seems you are a look-alike for someone they once knew."

She felt a sudden relief. So the explanation was as simple as that. She'd been making too much of it. She said, "So that was it!"

"Yes," he went on. "He didn't make it clear who the person was. But I listened to them discuss it among themselves when I was preparing the contract for rental and I gathered that it was a young woman they knew years ago. Someone now dead. And they seemed to think you bore a startling resemblance to her."

"Dead!" Aunt Samantha said sharply. "Did they mention any name?"

John considered a moment. "Come to think of it I did hear the woman say her name once. I'm not sure but I think it was June."

The casual words came like a thunderbolt for Vera. She gave her Aunt Samantha a quick look to see if the old woman remembered. And by the cunning expression on the lined, leathery face she knew that she did. For June was the name that had been spelled out for Samantha on the Ouija board the previous night. A message from that other world of phantoms!

CHAPTER THREE

Aunt Samantha said nothing but the look of grim satisfaction on her ancient face spoke more loudly than any words. Vera had been startled enough by the revelation that she resembled a dead friend of the Harper family without wanting to go into the grisly business of whether or not this had been predicted in a spirit's message. She firmly believed it was only a coincidence that the name June had turned up in both instances. And Aunt Samantha had not been sure whether the name she spelled out on the Ouija board had been June or Jane. Let it go at that.

She somehow managed to turn the conversation to something else. And dinner went by without any further reference to the Harpers. In line with her usual routine, Aunt Samantha left them early to go upstairs to her room. Vera guessed the old woman did not retire at once but instead spent long hours over her Ouija board or using some other means of communication with the spirit world.

When she and the young lawyer were finally left to sit and chat by themselves in the living room she ventured to bring up the Harpers once more.

"I still see them as an odd group," she told him. "It's as if there was some shadow over them that holds them together."

He smiled. "You are becoming almost as fanciful as your aunt."

"I hope not," she said with amused irony. "Still I am supposed to be taking some responsibility in the rentals. And I feel we should know more about these people before allowing them to have the house."

"I've already checked them through their bank," he said. "They have plenty of money."

"What else do you know about them?"

He shrugged. "What else should I know? You can tell they are solid upper middle class. There's usually not much exciting about such people."

She stared down at the rug pensively. "I still have a strange feeling about them."

"Because they stared at you. You know the reason for that now."

"I know what they told you."

"There's no cause to doubt that what they said is true," the young lawyer said with a hint of irritation in his voice. "I've occasionally found myself in the same awkward position. When you see someone who reminds you of somebody else you can't help staring. And if the person reminds you of a dead person the compulsion is often stronger."

Her eyes met his. "If this June I remind them of is dead, she must have died awfully young. I mean I'm not exactly old, am I?"

John Murchison eyed her approvingly. "You certainly are not. And I agree she must have died young and in her full beauty."

"They didn't tell you anything about her."

"No. They didn't discuss her directly with me at all. It was only by listening closely that I learned what I did. I think you're making far too much of it."

"Perhaps," she said with some reluctance. "But I do wish you could find out more of their background."

"I'll see if I can," he told her. But he didn't sound too concerned.

She sighed. "The thing is I'm not sure I'll like having them for neighbors. And Aunt Samantha may not approve of them."

"She'll probably think they're great," the lawyer said. "Don't forget Maria Harper is a spiritualism bug. That's the main reason she wants to live in the house."

"So she says."

"What other reason could there be?" John wanted to know. "And I thought you were bothered by the ghost of our lovely friend on the wall. You should be pleased that someone is moving into the Colonial house who may put her unhappy spirit to rest."

"I've somehow forgotten her and the legend for the moment," she admitted. "I'm thinking more about them."

"If you think of them at all," John Murchison said, "it should be with gratitude for their renting that white elephant of a house."

"They're probably only doing it because it suits them," she said.

He frowned. "Just what do you mean by that?"

"I think they have a special reason for wanting to live in it, beyond the ghost hunting which Maria Harper claims is their chief interest."

"Now that's morbid thinking. Isn't it possible they just like the house? It's a fine old place and we'd have sold it long ago if it didn't have such an evil reputation."

"They know all about its reputation and yet they want to come here to it," she said. "I find that peculiar for a start."

The young lawyer sat back on the divan and groaned. "Please, let's not worry about it any more. I thought when I came here with the good news you'd be delighted. Instead you've done nothing but give me a kind of crazy third degree."

"I'm sorry," she said, honestly contrite. She could see his side of it and wished she felt the same way. But it wasn't his fault that she didn't. In any case she was probably overdoing it. "I'll not mention the Harpers again tonight."

"Good," he said.

She gave him a teasing smile. "I would like an honest answer to one question."

"Go ahead."

"Is the fog here as bad as they claim?"

"Only for a few weeks in the spring and then briefly in the fall," he said. "I'd say we were beginning the foggy season now. So be prepared for a lot of it."

"Thanks for one direct and honest answer," she said with a tiny laugh.

The young lawyer looked happier. "I make a specialty of honest answers and questions. Now I'll ask you one."

"Well?"

"Do you like me?"

She was at once confused. It wasn't the sort of question she'd been expecting. She smiled, "Yes, I do."

"I'm glad. Because I like you."

There was a teasing light in her eyes. "Even if we are going to argue some about the rentals."

"That's going to be only a minor problem," he assured her. "The thing is you strike me as the type of girl I've been looking for. These last few years I've been giving ninety percent of my time to business and there hasn't been much chance for romance. Now I suddenly feel I've been missing out on a pretty important part of living."

"I've heard the idea rumored," she said demurely.

"All right," he said unhappily. "I've given you the story on me. I'm a bachelor with no strings and a lot of admiration for you. What about you? You're not wearing a ring so I take it you're fancy free as well?"

"At the moment," she said carefully. "I was going to be engaged. It might become an active romance again. He had to move away when he was promoted. I still hear from him but we're marking time."

"Keep on marking it," John urged her, taking her hand in his. "I'd like a little while to plead my case."

She smiled. "As a lawyer you should be an expert at it."

"I wish that were true," he said dolefully.

"When it comes to speaking for myself I never do so well."

"I think you manage very nicely."

John Murchison looked glum. "I get off to a fast start but I'm not good in the follow up. It's an old problem with me."

"At least you know your failing."

"That doesn't mean I can help it," he mourned. Then looking a little brighter, he added, "At least we've cleared the decks and made a start. After you've been here a few days I'd like to take you out to meet some young people. You can't stay cooped up here with Samantha. You're morbid enough as it is. That would finish you."

She laughed. "You needn't worry about that. And my aunt wants me to get out."

"So she says," the young lawyer said with a frown. "But what Samantha says and what she actually means aren't always the same. Watch out or she'll have you completely under her domination."

"There's no chance of my allowing anything like that."

"Just keep my warning in mind," he told her.

They talked some more and he told her about the country club and the Saturday night dances. It was more or less decided between them that she'd go to the next Saturday night event. Suddenly it was getting late and time for him to leave.

At the door she reminded him, "Try and get some more information on those Harpers."

He gave her a teasing look. "Surely they're not coming between us again?"

"I mean it," she insisted.

"And so do I," he said as he gently took her in his arms and gave her a first kiss. She'd been expecting some gesture on his part so it didn't come as a surprise nor did she resent it. She found herself liking the young lawyer and knew that she would have to depend on him a good deal in the days ahead. How much she didn't dream at this moment. But she relaxed in his embrace and returned his kiss.

John left in a good mood. And she felt more relaxed than she had for some time. In spite of some of the unsettling aspects of her coming to live with her aunt there was a promise of more pleasant times ahead. She closed the front door against the cold, heavy fog that was lasting through the night and turned toward the stairway. The house was silent and full of shadows. And as she began to ascend the stairs she found herself again thinking of the sad-faced beauty whose photograph hung in the hall and who had used those same stairs until the night when she went next door to be murdered.

In her bedroom the odd chill feeling of the unknown pressed in on her. And when she finally managed to sleep, she again had troubled dreams in which the long dead beauty plagued her. And now the faces of the Harpers joined in the nightmare. The dark-clad, thin trio had made a sinister impression on her. It was possible she was being unfair to them but she couldn't help feeling they offered some sort of weird menace.

She battled the nightmares that tormented her and the occasional fear she knew in the daytimes. A week passed in which she became more accustomed to the old mansion and the vagaries of her elderly aunt's disposition. John's warning had been a sound one. Gradually, just a little at a time, Aunt Samantha was revealing herself as something of a tyrant.

Positive proof of this came the next Saturday night — her first in Portland — when Vera announced she was going to the country club dance with John. The old woman disapproved and gave as her reason that she wasn't feeling well and required Vera's company. This led to Vera frankly telling her she wasn't going to be a twenty-four hour companion. That she expected to have a life of her own. In the end Samantha gave in meekly and allowed her to go out.

But the old woman infringed on her in other ways. She taunted her with the spiritualism in which she was always indulging. Samantha knew that it made Vera uneasy and delighted in going on about it in her presence. It seemed that each night the old woman received a new message on her Ouija board.

One morning she came down in an especially taunting mood and as soon as she was comfortably settled in her wheelchair told Vera, "I had another message concerning you last night."

Vera braced herself for what would follow, determined not to let the old invalid upset her. She said, "I can't imagine why your spirit friends should be worried about me."

"But they are!"

"I'm really not interested," she said, preparing to leave the old woman and go to one of the other rooms.

"Wait!" Aunt Samantha called out in a tone of command. And then leaning forward in the chair with her sunken eyes gleaming, she said, "That name came out on the board last night. June!"

"So?"

"You know about it," the old woman said with some annoyance. "Those Harpers discussed it with John. That's the name of the dead girl you reminded them of, June!"

"I'd forgotten," Vera pretended.

"I don't think so," the old woman said shifting in the wheelchair with a firmness in her tone. "No, I don't believe that at all. Whoever that June is she's trying to reach us here."

"I have no faith in your Ouija board."

"Then the more fool you," Aunt Samantha said hotly.

"I'm sure it's a case of your making the words you want come out on the board," Vera told her. "You may believe the spirits are directing your hands but I say it's your subconscious."

Rage showed on the leathery old face. "You'll never shake my faith in the board."

"And I'll never believe in what it says," Vera told her mildly. "So let's leave it at that. There's no reason why we should quarrel about it."

Aunt Samantha seemed to have second thoughts. She sank back in her chair and studied her gloomily. "You're an attractive, intelligent girl. I can't understand why you close your mind to the spirit world."

"I'm not denying it. I'm simply saying that I'm not as sensitive to it as you appear to be. And I don't like to hear about your messages from the other side all the time."

The old woman in the wheelchair sighed. "It's a case of your fighting your own nature. One of these days you'll admit it and then you'll bloom in full psychic glory! Your eyes will be opened!"

Vera smiled grimly. "I'm content to wait until then."

Aunt Samantha was at once turning her mind to other problems as she often did with no warning. Glaring in the direction of the living room window she said, "Another wet foggy day! Drat this weather."

"We are having a lot of it."

"One fine day since you arrived," the old woman reminded her. And then with an expression of concern on the lined, hawk face. "And the Harpers are due to move in tomorrow. They've already sent one truckload of things ahead."

"The house is ready for them, isn't it?"

"I've had Mrs. Gaskell supervise two girls in uncovering the furniture and cleaning up the place," her aunt said. "And the furnace is on to keep out the dampness. I wish you'd go over and make a check to see that everything has been properly taken care of."

Vera suddenly felt a recurrence of some of the old fear. She asked her aunt, "It's definite the Harpers are coming tomorrow?"

"Yes."

"John didn't mention it to me," she said quietly. And he hadn't. He'd been careful to avoid any discussion of the Boston family. And because of this she was positive he'd not done as she'd asked. He'd not made any other inquiries about them. Perhaps his decision not to do this had been right. But she still wondered.

"I think you should go over there this morning and see the house is in proper shape for them," Aunt Samantha said. "After all it is your responsibility."

"Very well," she said. "I'll go in a little while."

She put it off until after lunchtime. And then when she knew her aunt was about to begin nagging her again she put on her raincoat and tied a kerchief around her hair. She already had the extra key to the Colonial house so she went out into the gray fog of the miserable spring day. It was wet underfoot as well and she picked her way between puddles as she hurried to the imposing white house.

It took her only a moment to unlock the

door and then she was inside and alone in the almost frightening quiet of the deserted house. She stood there in the high-ceilinged living room with its fine antique furnishings and thought of all the terrifying legends that had been told about its ghosts. How the house itself had taken on a sinister power that twisted the lives of all those who came to live in it.

Yet the Harpers were ready and even somewhat anxious to make this their home. Why? She couldn't think of any satisfactory reason. She moved slowly from room to room behaving like some silent phantom herself. She gave a wry smile as this thought crossed her mind. She took note of the condition of all the rooms and it seemed to her that Mrs. Gaskell had supervised the work well. With the lower floor taken care of she decided to move on upstairs.

She was almost to the top of the stairs when the furnace far down in the cellar came on suddenly and a kind of vibration went through the old house. It gave her a start and she halted and gripped the bannister fiercely as she stared over its railing into the deep shadows below. Of course it was only the furnace. She was being ridiculous allowing such things to bother her. With a deep sigh she resumed ascending the stairs.

Reaching the landing she halted. She knew that she was now somewhere near the room in which the long ago tragedy had taken place. The room must be on her right and near the end of the hall if its window could be seen from the other house. And on that fatal night the unhappy two had kept their rendezvous in that room. Shots and frenzied screams had rung out to bring the curtain down on the lives of the lovers.

How many times had the two come up these very stairs? And did they still return to stalk the shadowy passages as silent phantoms? According to one story their death screams could still be heard on certain nights. Cold fingers of fear began to close around Vera's heart. She stood there motionless at the head of the stairs for several minutes before she found the courage to move on.

Then she began her inspection of the bedrooms beginning on the opposite side of the house from the death room. Some of her fright drained away from her as she gave her attention to the details of the housekeeping in each room. But she knew that eventually she must cross to the other murkily lighted room where violent death had left its mark. They said the bullet holes of the gun used that night were still in the walls. They had been papered over but never filled in and if you ran your hand over the wall you could still feel them. She tried to push such unsettling thoughts from her mind.

She was foolish to allow Aunt Samantha's spiritualism to get on her nerves this way. She must keep calm. But the picture of that sad face of the murdered beauty was etched on her brain. And as she neared the room which she knew must have been the scene of the suicide and murder she almost pictured the lovely form standing in the shadows of the doorway blocking her from entering. But as she came close to the doorway the illusion vanished as most phantoms were wont to do. Trembling but triumphant she forced herself to enter the room and stare around it. There was a double bed and a dresser in there and not much else. An ordinary enough room to have known such dark secrets.

She moved slowly across to the window and drew back the curtain so that she could look at Aunt Samantha's Tudor mansion. She was able to pick out the room she occupied and which had once belonged to the murdered beauty. She was still staring out into the dull light of the late, fog-ridden afternoon when something else impinged on her consciousness. At first she couldn't believe it. And then she went rigid as she became aware of a heavy breathing close to her!

The shadowed room was deserted and yet she continued to hear this somewhat tortured but regular breathing almost in her ear. Very slowly she turned to look behind her and then she realized she was standing almost directly in front of a clothes closet. And the closet door was opening very gradually. The sight of this made her cry out! And now she raced from the room and made for the carpeted stairs.

She screamed again with the sureness that rapid footsteps were following her. Phantom footsteps! She was more than a third way down the stairs when her heel caught in the carpeting and she stumbled forward with her hands sprawled before her. She knew she was taking a bad fall and screamed once more as she tried to protect herself. Then she fainted.

When she opened her eyes she was stretched out on the floor of the hallway, there was a dull ache in her shoulder and head, and a tall, dark figure was standing by her. The figure knelt beside her.

"I'm terribly sorry I frightened you, Miss Waters," the man in dark was saying in a voice that sounded vaguely familiar. And then she got a glimpse of his face and recognized him.

"William Harper," she said, naming the older bachelor brother as she studied his angular face with wary eyes.

"Yes. Are you badly hurt?"

She raised herself up on the side opposite the aching shoulder. "I don't think so," she said. "My shoulder is paining and my head, too. I don't think it's anything."

"I certainly hope not," the thin man said in a distressed tone. "It was stupid of me to give you such a scare."

She was staring at him. "Was it you in that room?"

"Yes. Just before you came in I'd entered the closet. I realized that I might upset you by emerging suddenly. At first I decided just to wait in there until you'd gone. Then I planned to catch up with you in the hallway in a normal manner."

Fear still was written on her pretty face. "I heard your breathing and then I saw the door open slowly."

William Harper grimaced. "My stupid solution to the situation. I decided if I came out slowly it wouldn't be such a shock to you."

"I thought you were a ghost."

"A logical assumption. You were alone in

a deserted house. You had no reason to believe I'd be there."

"I knew no one else had a key," she said. "And you people weren't expected until tomorrow."

He nodded. "I know. I decided to come down ahead of the others."

"I see," she said. Her head was still throbbing dully but the aching in her shoulder had almost vanished.

"Do you feel able to stand?" he asked solicitously.

"Yes," she said and made an effort. He quickly came to her assistance and a moment later she was rather shakily on her feet in the shadowed hallway. The thin man in the black suit was a full head taller than she was.

"I assume you were over here checking on the house," he said.

"Yes. My aunt thought I should."

"Very kind of her," William Harper said pleasantly. "I feel very guilty about this incident. I hope you'll forgive me."

"It's all right," she said, conscious of his shrewd eyes boring into her. His penetrating glance served to bring back the old nervousness.

"Forgive my staring," he apologized. "But you remind me of someone who was very dear to me."

"Oh?" She'd heard this from John Murchison of course but didn't feel she should let on.

"A young woman long since dead," William Harper went on. "Your likeness to her is startling."

"I see," she said not knowing how to reply.

"We all noticed it when we first saw you the other day," William Harper went on in his dry voice. "I'm afraid we must have made you somewhat aware of our interest."

She smiled wanly. "As long as the resemblance doesn't make you feel uncomfortable."

The effect of her words on the tall, thin man was startling. His eyes opened wide as he asked her, "Why did you say that?"

"What?"

"That the resemblance might make some one of us upset."

She was shocked by the concern in his voice. She'd actually meant nothing in particular. And she couldn't understand why he should make so much of it. She said, "It was just a reply. I don't think I meant anything special. Or if I did I was wondering if my looking like your dead friend might bring you sad memories."

He almost visibly relaxed. A sigh escaped

from him. "Of course. That is very thoughtful of you. You are a sensitive person."

"My aunt seems to think so."

"And I agree," William Harper said in too warm a manner. All his attitudes were somewhat exaggerated. It seemed typical of him. She decided he must be an extremely nervous type.

She said, "I'll tell Aunt Samantha you're here."

"Please do."

She had an urge to get away from the house and be rid of his tense presence. Edging a step toward the front door, she said, "You'll be remaining in the house until your brother and his wife arrive tomorrow."

He smiled sadly. "Yes. So if you see lights in the windows and a figure moving about don't put it down to ghosts."

Vera felt ashamed of the display of nerves she'd given. "I won't," she said. "And I can't imagine why I behaved so badly upstairs. I guess I've listened too much to the spooky stories about this place."

"Quite understandable," he assured her. "We'll say nothing more about it." He hesitated. "Where were you born, Miss Waters?"

It struck her as an odd question. But she said, "In Boston."

"Your parents are still living?"

"In Florida. They moved there when my father retired."

The eyes of the thin man were fastened on her again. "Many people do," he agreed. And then very tactfully he went on, "I'm not sure but I have an idea your lawyer friend mentioned that you were adopted. That you are Mrs. Waters's adopted niece."

Vera eyed him incredulously. "I don't know what could have made him say that. He's wrong."

The older Harper brother was at once apologetic again. "I can't think why I got that impression," he said. "But then I'm always mixing things up. So please don't blame the young man. He probably didn't say it at all."

She could have replied that John Murchison certainly hadn't said any such thing. But it was too obvious that the thin man had been sounding her out on his own for some reason. It was he who'd wanted to make sure of her parentage. But why?

She touched her hand to the doorknob. "If there's anything you need just call us at the other house."

"I'll do that," he promised. "Thank you for coming over."

She opened the door and stepped out into

the dampness and fog. It was darker than it should have been even for this time in the late afternoon. As she quickly went down the steps to the sidewalk her eyes wandered to the opposite side of the dead-end street and she saw a man in a raincoat with a soft felt hat slouched over his face standing there in the fog watching her.

It gave her a start because no one came into the short street unless they had some business there or lived there. And the people in the other occupied house were off somewhere on vacation according to her aunt. Yet this man was loitering in the gray mist and seemingly spying on her. Or at least watching the house. She pretended not to see him and hurried along the sidewalk to her aunt's place. She went inside without glancing across the street again. But once in the safety of the Tudor house she peered out one of the small windows and saw that the intruder had vanished.

CHAPTER FOUR

The somewhat eerie sequence of events of the foggy afternoon made a strong impression on Vera. She didn't care to confide her feelings of uneasiness to her Aunt Samantha who would undoubtedly at once put it all down to the spirits, so she decided to contact John Murchison and talk to him at the first opportunity. It was daily more clear to her that her dependence on the young lawyer was going to be great.

That evening she had the strange experience of staring across at the Colonial house and seeing lights at its windows for the first time since she'd come to live in Portland. Aunt Samantha had been interested to hear that William Harper had come ahead of the others and questioned her a good deal about him.

At last Vera said, "I don't understand why you don't invite him over here to meet you."

The old woman in the wheelchair looked crafty. "I can do without that," she said. "I want you to make all the contact with these people. It will be good experience for you."

"They may think it odd that you avoid them. Especially the woman who is apparently as much interested in spiritualism as you."

The shrewd lined face of Aunt Samantha revealed a faint smile. "If I see her it will be in my own good time. Meanwhile my being an invalid excuses me from the tiresome business of greeting them. You will find it best not to make close friends of tenants."

Vera looked at her in bewilderment. "But you have forced me to see a lot of these people."

"As yet you are not the landlord," her aunt reminded her dryly. "You are merely my agent."

"I have found the Harpers unusual and hard to know," she said. "I'm not sure I like them."

"Has there been any more mention of that June?" her aunt wanted to know.

She gave her an odd look. "No names were mentioned," she said. "But William Harper did repeat that I looked like a dead girl who had been close and dear to his family."

Aunt Samantha was leaning forward in the wheelchair with an expression of avid attention, as if she were afraid of missing some important word. "Is that what he said?"

"Something like that. I can't recall his exact words."

The ancient eyes glittered at her. "Perhaps he is thinking it could be a case of transmigration."

She frowned. "Transmigration?"

"Is the word unknown to you?"

"I'm afraid so," she admitted cautiously; she knew at once that she was being baited into another discussion of some phase of the spirit world.

The old woman clutched the arms of her wheelchair. "If you weren't so obstinate about such things I'd have explained it to you before now. It's part of my spiritualism which you despise."

"I don't feel anything about it at all," she protested. "You are welcome to believe what you like. And so, I trust, am I."

Aunt Samantha smiled grimly. "You don't fool me, young woman. I know where you stand on the subject. But for your information transmigration is the transference of the soul of some dead person to the body of a living one. An aging relative dies and at once seeks out an infant of the same blood and takes over its body. And in due time the child grows to be very like the deceased."

"I find that horrible!"

Aunt Samantha chuckled. "I think that it

happens. And can happen to older folk as well. The point being that the person occupied by the spirit gradually grows to resemble the spirit and even the similar physical likeness becomes pronounced."

Vera was shaken by the old woman's words but she kept her attitude of defiance. "I call it just another ghost story and a revolting one."

"Transmigration has been accepted as a truth down through the centuries," the woman in the wheelchair told her calmly. "So how do you know that years ago you weren't taken possession of by the wandering spirit of this dead June?"

In spite of the fact she considered the statement fantastic Vera still felt a thrill of fear sweep through her. "If you continue to go on in this way I'm returning to Boston," she threatened.

This brought a reaction from Aunt Samantha. The old woman raised a lean, protesting hand. "Don't say that," she quavered. "I'm sorry I offended you. Having you here has been such a comfort to me. Please forgive the meanderings of a silly, lonely old woman!"

Vera thought the apology too contrite to be entirely sincere. But she knew that her aunt had indeed been lonely and no doubt this was why she had turned to spiritualism for comfort in this twisted way.

She said, “I think it’s important you understand my feelings.”

“I do,” Aunt Samantha assured her.

An uneasy truce was thus declared between them. But Vera was on edge for her meeting with John Murchison the following day. When she’d called and asked for an appointment the young lawyer had suggested they have luncheon together at a downtown hotel and combine business with pleasure. She agreed to meet him there at twelve-thirty.

She felt it was important she have a talk with him before the other Harpers arrived. And so she spent another uneasy night waiting for the meeting with him. The next day was sunny and a lot warmer. She began to feel that spring in Maine mightn’t be such a dismal season after all. But she also knew it could merely be an exception. In any event it made the prospect of her luncheon with John more pleasant.

Vera had been keeping her car parked in the rear of the Tudor house and now she used it to drive downtown for her appointment with John. She found the business streets of the old city as busy and twisting as the ancient sections of Boston. At last she located the hotel and a suitable parking space. Then she went inside to find the young lawyer.

He was waiting for her at the door of the dining room. His boyish face lit with a smile on seeing her. "You're a remarkable female," he said. "You're punctual."

"Mostly by accident," she smiled.

They went into the somewhat dark interior of the fashionable dining room and were shown to a suitably remote table for two. They were in a corner which gave them a view of the other diners and a degree of privacy. After John had ordered he turned to study her with a look of tolerant amusement.

"So what are all your problems?" he asked.

"I have plenty."

"Sounds grim. Such as?"

"Aunt Samantha for a beginning. She will harp on spiritualism. All that ghost talk isn't doing my nerves any good."

"Think of the money she's leaving you."

"Not even that makes me want to remain with her."

"She needs you. She's old, lonely, and none too well."

Vera smiled thinly. "Those are better arguments."

He was watching her closely. "I think you're a rather remarkable young woman.

I'm glad we've met. But then I've told you that before."

"You have," she said. "Did you find out anything more about the Harpers?"

"Their check for the lease didn't bounce."

She frowned. "You didn't expect it to, did you?"

He spread his hands. "Who knows? You don't seem to have a high opinion of them."

"That is true," was her reply. "But my judgment of them isn't based on their financial circumstances. I'm sure they have plenty of money. I'd be more interested in how they came by it."

"Old family. Inherited."

"They don't strike me as old family," she said. "And I've been exposed to a lot of them in Boston. There is something unsure in their manner. Haven't you noticed that?"

"I'm afraid not."

She regarded him with slight annoyance. "Because you don't want to," she said. "You're so interested in renting that house and getting your money you don't think of anything else."

"What else is there?"

"They could be the wrong kind of people."

He smiled. "You're not becoming a snob, I trust."

"I'm not becoming a snob," she said acidly. "But I have found the Harpers strange from the beginning. And I do blame you for not finding more information concerning them than their bank balance."

John looked bothered for the first time. "I didn't think it meant that much to you. That you were really worried."

"I am," she said. And then as an example of what she felt and why she told him about her visit to the Colonial house the previous afternoon and her weird encounter with William Harper.

John heard her out and said, "You can't blame William Harper because your nerves were in a state."

"I don't think he behaved in a completely normal fashion either," she maintained. "And what did all that talk about my being adopted mean?"

"Nothing. I certainly didn't say anything like that. Harper probably told you the truth when he said he had his facts mixed up."

Her eyes met his. "I think there is more to it than that."

"Such as?"

"I'm not sure," she said earnestly. "But I have an idea it has a lot to do with Maria Harper's obsession with spiritualism. There's something unhealthful in the way they harp on my likeness to that dead girl."

John didn't look impressed. "I think that was only mentioned in passing. You shouldn't emphasize it so."

"Before they came over to the house and met me, had they made any definite decision about the rental?"

"No, they hadn't," the young lawyer said with some surprise.

"But after they saw me and noticed my resemblance to the dead girl they refer to as June, they made up their minds quickly about renting."

"I wouldn't call it a quick decision," he objected. "And it's quite usual for prospective tenants not to make up their minds until the final discussion at my office. I don't think it had anything to do with your likeness to their dead friend."

She smiled bleakly. "That's your theory but I will stay with mine."

Lunch was served and the talk turned to other things. Not until they were having dessert and coffee did John Murchison bring up the subject of rentals again. Then he had a new bit of information.

"I have a man interested in the cottage," he said. "He's about ready to sign the lease. He's also a retired bachelor of about middle age. He was in civil service or something like that and he's looking for a quiet place to live."

"He should find our street ideal."

John nodded. "That's what I told him. He looks a good, solid type. Do you want to meet him before he signs the lease?"

"No," she said. "Entertaining the Harpers was ordeal enough. I'm sure we can trust your judgment on this. Rent the cottage to your man if you think he is all right. What's his name? Aunt Samantha will want to know."

The young lawyer took a small black notebook from an inner pocket and consulted it. "His name is Henry Eden. He had a house in Cambridge which he recently sold. Just now he's living in a motel on the outskirts of town."

"I'll tell Aunt Samantha," she said. "I know she'll be happy that all the places are rented. When will this Henry Eden be moving in?"

"Probably as soon as I settle the details with him, I'll let you know."

They left the restaurant shortly after and he walked her to the parking lot and her car in the warm sunlight of the spring afternoon. She felt relaxed and almost forgot her concern about the Harpers for a little time.

It was as she was about to enter her car

that she remembered something else. And with a puzzled expression on her attractive face she said, "There is one other thing. When I came out of the Colonial house yesterday there was a man standing across the street watching the house. Someone I'd never seen before and we don't have people loitering around the street."

John smiled at her tolerantly. "Surely you're not trying to make anything of that?"

"It gave me a creepy feeling," she said. "I have an idea he was watching that house and me. When I got back to Aunt Samantha's I looked out the window and he had gone. But he seemed mysterious standing there in the fog."

The lawyer laughed. "He was probably some salesman debating whether you might be a prospect."

"I don't know," she worried. "He had an air about him. A kind of sinister manner. I couldn't see his face because of the distance and the fog. But I have an idea he was there watching because of the Harpers."

"Nonsense."

"Maybe," she said ruefully. "But I wish we knew more about them."

They parted on this note. John promising to phone her soon about a date. And she drove back to the rambling pseudo-Tudor house on the quiet side street at least knowing the satisfaction of having talked out her troubles to someone. If the young lawyer hadn't been entirely sympathetic, at least he'd listened to her.

Aunt Samantha was in the big living room in her wheelchair waiting for her. Even on a bright day like this the interior of the house was still dark and gloomy. She went in to sit down with her aunt for a moment before going upstairs.

"Did you have a pleasant luncheon?" the old woman asked.

"Very," she said.

"You like John?"

She smiled. "He's very nice. And he told me he has a tenant for the cottage. A bachelor named Henry Eden. He's some kind of retired civil servant."

The lined face of her aunt brightened. "That's good news," she said. "I dislike having the properties here empty. They deteriorate so much more quickly when no one is in them and it makes the street lonely."

"I thought you'd be pleased," Vera said.

"A man called here to see you when you were out," the old woman in the wheelchair informed her.

Vera was surprised. "Was it William

Harper? I told him to phone or drop in if there was anything needed for the other house."

"No. It wasn't Harper. Mrs. Gaskell asked him about that."

"Then who was it?"

"He wouldn't leave his name," Aunt Samantha said. "But he promised that he would call back another time."

"When?"

"He didn't say that either."

Vera frowned. "I can't imagine who it could be." Then she suddenly recalled the mysterious stranger she'd seen across the street watching her the previous afternoon. The man John had suggested was probably a salesman. And she said, "I saw a man across the street yesterday. I think he was selling something. It was probably him."

The shrewd eyes in the ancient leathery face showed a blank expression. "I couldn't say," her aunt murmured. "But I thought I should tell you."

"I wonder if the other two Harpers have arrived yet?" she asked.

"I don't know," Aunt Samantha said.

But Vera was to find out that they had come before the day ended. A phone call came in the late afternoon and it was Maria Harper on the line. The frail woman sounded in a friendly mood.

"We're settled in," she said. "And I know I'm going to adore it here. We were all wondering if you might come by for a drink with us after dinner tonight?"

Vera hesitated. She had no wish to join the Harpers whom she still didn't fully understand or trust but she didn't want to appear stand-offish on their first night in the Colonial house. She quickly debated what she could do to get gracefully out of it.

She said, "You must be weary. Some other time might be better."

"No. We'd really like to have you tonight," the older woman insisted.

She hesitated again. Then reluctantly said, "Well, perhaps for just a short while. I plan to go to bed early tonight."

"Fine," the frail woman sounded pleased. "Shall we say around nine then?"

"Nine will be all right," Vera agreed. And she put down the phone with a frown wondering why she'd allowed herself to be so easily talked into a visit she anticipated only with distaste.

Aunt Samantha showed surprise when she heard about it. "I thought you planned to keep your distance with the Harpers," she said.

Vera had donned a psychedelic multicolored cut velvet dress for the visit next door and now stood before her aunt somewhat guiltily. "I do mean to," she said. "But the Harper woman was very pressing in her invitation and I didn't want to appear rude."

A peculiar smile flickered at the sunken corners of the old invalid's mouth. "Perhaps this way you'll get to know them better and be less critical of them."

"Perhaps."

Aunt Samantha gave her a taunting look. "I'll spend the evening with my Ouija board and maybe the spirits will tell me more than you'll learn. Though I know you won't believe that."

"I'll be back as early as I can," Vera said, deliberately ignoring her aunt's reference to spiritualism.

When she stepped outside she found that the temperature had dropped a good deal since the daytime. And she was glad she had slipped on a topcoat. She quickly made her way to the Colonial house and rang the doorbell. As she waited for the door to be answered she turned and casually glanced across the street. What she saw made her suddenly go tense. Standing there in the shadows away from the single street lamp was the same man she'd seen the day before.

"Good evening, Miss Waters." It was William Harper who had opened the door and was greeting her cordially.

She turned to him with troubled eyes and asked, "That man standing over there across the street. Do you know him?"

William Harper frowned slightly and looked in the direction she'd indicated. "What man?"

"Right over there," she said wheeling around again. But to her dismay she saw there was no one in sight. He had vanished into the shadows.

"I see no one," the thin, dark man said in a tone mixing curiosity with quiet surprise.

She felt embarrassed. "I must have been mistaken," she murmured. And she went inside. But she knew a man had been standing there.

William Harper took her coat and then guided her into the living room where James Harper and his wife, Maria, were waiting for her. Maria came forward to greet her with a smile on the sad face with the dark-circled eyes.

"It was good of you to come," she said warmly. "It will help us adjust to these new surroundings."

The weakly handsome James Harper also greeted her and then mixed her the small whiskey and soda which she requested. She sat with Maria on a large divan and the two men took easy chairs opposite them. When they were all seated William Harper brought up the subject of the man across the street.

"Miss Waters thought there was someone standing across the street either watching her or this house," he said in his dry voice. "I couldn't see anyone but that doesn't mean no one was there."

James Harper shot his brother a knowing glance. "It certainly does not," he said. And he gave his attention to Vera. "Can you describe this person?"

"Not really," she said, trying to remember. "I'd guess he was of medium size and build. His hat was drawn down over his face so I didn't get a good look at him."

William Harper's angular face was grim. "I can say one thing. He vanished in a hurry."

Vera thought she should make it clear she hadn't imagined the whole incident. She said, "I saw him once before. The day I came here to the house. He was standing over there then. And he vanished quickly in the same way he did tonight."

Maria Harper uttered a tiny gasp of dismay. "I hope it's not going to start all over again!"

This cryptic statement left Vera baffled. She studied the faces of the three in the short silence that followed the frail woman's distressed outburst and saw that all three wore expressions of concern. And she realized at once there might be a good deal more to this than she'd guessed.

It was the older of the two brothers who offered her the first hint of an explanation in his dry fashion. "I don't think we've mentioned it before," he told her. "But one of the chief reasons we moved from Boston was because of a certain harassment we'd been experiencing there."

"A harassment?" she questioned.

"Yes," he said grimly. "It's a fairly common thing today from what we've been able to learn. Some crackpot decides to institute a vitriolic campaign against a family of relative wealth and does so using the telephone, the mails, any means by which he can be a nuisance."

Maria Harper's face was ashen. "It can't begin again here," she protested. "I couldn't stand it."

William Harper frowned at his sister-in-law. "There's no reason to suppose it will," he told her sternly. "There probably is a perfectly harmless explanation for this man Miss Waters has seen."

James Harper got to his feet with a look of exasperation on that too handsome and somewhat feminine face. "My wife has good reason to feel the way she does," he said angrily. "If that hate campaign begins again here we have wasted all the effort and expense of making this move!"

Vera stared up at him. "You came here because of someone annoying you?"

"It was more than mere annoyance," James Harper said, thoroughly upset now. "My brother has a tendency to understate. We were under constant pressure of obscene and threatening phone calls and then almost every day we received some insane, accusing note in the mail."

Maria Harper gave her a distressed glance. "You have no idea how such a thing builds up. It got so bad I hated to pick up the phone."

Vera looked at them all in bewilderment. "Surely the police and the phone people could help you?"

William Harper looked bitter. "Oh, we complained to them," he said. "Don't think we didn't. And they promised to investigate. And for a while they had a tracer on our phone. Of course during that period no calls came. But soon afterward they resumed again."

"No one was able to help us," James Harper said. "And no one seemed to care too much."

She was caught up in their concern. So she asked, "What sort of threats and calls were made?"

Again that rather pointed silence came to the group. The three Harpers looked white and uncomfortable. And she had the certain feeling that they would reveal nothing further. That they would probably lie to her about the nature of the calls. And once again her strong suspicions about them came surging back. It seemed to her this thin, intense middle-aged trio shared some monstrous secret or guilt.

Maria Harper finally broke the silence by telling her, "We'll not burden you with what this madman said to us. But I can promise you it was cruel and obscene. There should be some way to protect decent people against such twisted minds."

"I knew from the start running off here was no solution," her husband said, pacing back and forth in his upset.

From his chair William Harper gave his brother a bleak glance. "You've forgotten the most important fact," he reminded him. "Since we've arrived here there have been no calls or anything else to suggest that we're going to be subject to that nuisance again. And there is nothing to link all that with the man Miss Waters thinks she saw."

Vera felt she should try to dispel some of the tension her statement had brought about and so said, "It's quite possible it is a salesman of some kind. My aunt said that someone called to see me this afternoon when I was out. I wouldn't be upset about it."

William Harper's angular face showed approval. "I think you are right, Miss Waters." He gave the others a scathing glance. "I wouldn't have mentioned it at all if I'd known I was going to create such a panic."

The younger James Harper at once seemed to regain control of his feelings. With a forced smile he sank into the easy chair and said, "Forgive my making such a scene, Miss Harper. I'm afraid I have an emotional nature."

Maria spoke up in too bright a manner to be normal. "I always tell my husband he should have taken up the stage as a profession."

James Harper spread his hands in a gesture of resignation. "When one has a good deal of money it curbs ambition. I daresay I could have been a success in the theater."

Now the conversation turned to a discussion of recent plays and movies. Vera felt better in the changed, more relaxed mood of the group. Yet she still had the feeling that they were putting on a performance for her, that she had not been admitted to their confidence.

All at once Maria Harper was discussing spiritualism and she told Vera, "This house is fascinating. I'm sure it is teeming with ghosts."

William Harper offered his sister-in-law a reproving smile. "I don't think you should stimulate Miss Waters's imagination on that point. I'm sure she is nervous enough about this place as it is."

Vera blushed, knowing that he was referring to her panic of the other day. And she wondered if he had told the others. She said, "I try to avoid thinking of what happened here as much as I can."

"I suppose that is normal unless you have the special interest in the spirit world that some of us have," Maria said with a fervent look on her frail face. "I'm looking forward to meeting your aunt; I understand she is a believer."

Vera said, "Perhaps later. At the moment she's not feeling too well and not up to receiving visitors. She's very old."

"I understand," Maria said with sympathy.

Vera glanced at her wristwatch. "It's getting late. I really must go." And she got up from the divan.

The others rose as well. And Maria said, "Before you go there's something I must show you." And she quickly left her to go across to a table on the other side of the room.

William Harper said, "I think I know what my sister-in-law wants you to see. You will be impressed."

Maria came back with a silver framed small photograph which she'd taken from the table. Handing it to her, she said, "This is the last photo we had of June. You see we weren't just talking when we spoke about the likeness between you."

Vera took the framed photo and studied it. And there was no question that the blond girl in it looked enough like her to be a twin. Allowing for the change in hairstyles and clothing in the passage of twenty years, she saw that her features were almost identical with the dead girl's!

CHAPTER FIVE

Without looking up from the photograph Vera knew that they were all watching her intently for a reaction. She could sense it in the sudden silence. After a long moment she raised her eyes and saw the expectant look on the frail Maria's face. She returned the framed photographer to her.

"She does look like me," she said.

"Yes," Maria said with a sigh.

"Well, we mustn't be morbid about it," William Harper said sharply. "I'll see you back to your door, Miss Waters. We can't have you walking outside alone when it's possible that man you saw is still in the neighborhood."

"I'm sure there's no danger," she said.

The younger brother, James Harper, gave her a look of warning. "I agree with William," he said. "Best not to take chances."

So reluctantly she allowed the thin, dark-suited William to accompany her to the front door of her aunt's house. As soon as they were outside he glanced across the street for some sign of the loiterer. But there was no one in sight.

She said, "I'm sure I made too much of seeing that man. I don't think you need worry about it."

"I won't," he assured her as they walked along the sidewalk. "It is my brother and sister-in-law who became emotional over this matter. You mustn't pay too much attention to them."

She was surprised to hear him speak of them in this somewhat disparaging manner. She said, "Maria seems a fine, sincere person."

"But morbid," William Harper said. "You saw how she dwelt on June's picture and your likeness to it."

Vera asked, "Who was this June? And when did she die?"

The thin man at her side cleared his throat. "She died in an accident twenty years ago. A tragic business. Her name was June Amory."

"Was she related to you?"

Something like a deep sigh came from him. "She was my niece and James's of course. And Maria knew her well since she was only a year or so older than June and had married James not too long before June's death."

"How sad that this girl should die so

young." She tried to make it casual but she was experiencing a tautness of nerves. She felt that she was only hearing the part of the story he could bear to tell.

"We have always felt that way about her death," William Harper agreed as they reached the entrance to her aunt's place. "Even though June's father had only been our half-brother, we were very fond of the girl."

"Naturally."

"But these things happen," William went on. "And I see no point in making a fetish of death as my sister-in-law has. I believe that Maria's great interest in the spirit world began with June's death."

"Has she ever felt she reached her?"

The thin man scowled. "Several professional spiritualists have professed to speak for June at seances but Maria has never had any direct messages from her. Yet she still hopes."

"My aunt counts on the Ouija board for such contacts."

"Maria induces herself to enter a kind of trance," William Harper said with some disdain. "She thinks that the atmosphere of a house is very important in making contact with the other world. And that is why she sought out a house reputed to be haunted when we decided to move."

"I see," she said. "On the theory that she may get through to the spirits more easily."

"That appears to be the idea," he agreed. "Where there is a congregation of lost souls it should be easier to search out one. Calling on the phantoms of the man and woman who died so tragically over there, she thinks she may be able to get through to June. I have no patience with the idea."

"I suppose one should be sympathetic," Vera suggested. "In a way this turning to spiritualism is an expression of loneliness and grief."

William Harper's eyes were fixed on her. "You are extremely perceptive," he said.

"Not really," she said with a faint smile. "Thank you for seeing me safely home."

"I consider it an obligation, Miss Waters," the thin man said. "I trust we'll see each other more often now that we are neighbors."

Vera said good night to him and went inside and up to bed. The session at the house next door had left her thoughts in a whirl. There had been a strangeness in the atmosphere over there she could not quite understand. While she was certain the three shared some secret, she couldn't decide what it might be. Though she felt it must have something to do with the dead girl whose photo she had seen. Their niece June Amory who had died twenty years ago.

When Vera got up the following morning she saw that it was raining. The downpour was heavy and didn't let up. With the memories of the previous night still in her mind, she found herself restless and troubled. And when her aunt came down on the stairway elevator the old woman merely added to her uneasiness.

Sitting forward in the wheelchair with a questioning look on her wrinkled face, Samantha said, "How did you make out next door?"

She stood a distance from the old woman and glanced out the window at the rain as she answered. "It was all right."

"Do you still find them odd?"

"They're very different."

"Did they tell you anything else about that dead girl you're supposed to look like?"

"Only that she was a niece."

Aunt Samantha propelled her chair toward Vera and then with a triumphant smile on her leathery face, she said, "I can tell you something about her. She died in 1949."

Frowning at her, Vera said, "But I think I told you that. At least I said she'd died about twenty years ago."

The old woman in the wheelchair shook her head. "I didn't hear it from you at all. I worked it out on the Ouija board last night. She sent the message through to me. And I'll warrant there'll be others."

Vera didn't care to argue with her aunt. But she was almost certain she had mentioned the date of June Amory's death to her. Still the old woman was evidently ready to deny it. She preferred to believe that she had mystical powers.

After lunch the rain slacked and then the fog moved in once more. The foghorn on the point began to blast in its monotonous fashion and Vera saw that they were in for another miserable day. Once when she was standing by a side window she saw William Harper emerge from the house next door and get into the compact sedan parked in the driveway and head off in the direction of downtown. It made her wonder what the others were doing in the old house and how they spent their days.

Aunt Samantha went upstairs for her afternoon rest and Vera sat down in the living room with a book. She'd not heard from John and hoped he would soon call her and let her know what he'd done about renting the cottage. She also felt a desire to see him and enjoy his company. It seemed that it was only when she was with him that she could relax.

She was growing to like the young lawyer more at every meeting. He was somewhat on the unimaginative side and too apt to brush off things for which he had no answer as unimportant but aside from that she felt he was very nice. And he had expressed himself as being fond of her.

She read for about an hour and then her restlessness took over again. Getting up she moved around the big living room, hesitating by a window to stare out at the fog-ridden street, or stopping to examine some fine piece of furniture. Until at last she came to a halt before the oval, enlarged photograph of the sad beauty who'd lived in this house and died next door at the hand of her lover. The gilt frame set off the lovely face and Vera stared at the slightly-blurred enlargement and wondered about this woman who had moved so directly into tragedy. Had she guessed what her unhappy romance with the married man next door would lead to?

Vera was standing staring at the picture and pondering on these thoughts when the front doorbell suddenly rang. It made her jump since it came unexpectedly and with an unusual shrillness. Or perhaps she felt this because she'd been so absorbed with the picture of the murdered beauty and her thoughts concerning her.

She turned and started toward the front door. But Mrs. Gaskell got there first. She heard the door open and the exchange between the housekeeper and some male. A moment later the sullen Mrs. Gaskell came into the living room.

"There's a gentleman wishes to see you," she said.

"Who is it?"

"He didn't give me his name," the housekeeper said stolidly. "He's waiting in the hall."

"Do you know what he wants?"

"No. He said it was personal."

"Very well, I'll speak with him," Vera said. The housekeeper nodded in her grim way and went off to the rear of the house. Vera moved into the shadowed hallway and thought for a moment her caller must have changed his mind and left. Then she saw a movement in the corner of the nearly dark reception hall and the figure of a middle-aged man in a dark raincoat took shape in the gloom.

"Good afternoon, Miss Waters," he said with a pleasant smile. He had a square, tanned face and was graying at the temples. Not tall, he was broad shouldered and stocky in build. And she caught her breath as she realized that he had to be the same man she'd seen standing across the street watching her on those several occasions.

"I've seen you before," she said in nervous haste.

Hat in hand, he continued to smile at her. "I don't believe we've ever met. My name is Henry Eden."

"We've never met socially," she agreed. "But I've seen you. On the other side of the street. You were standing watching the house next door it seemed."

His eyebrows rose. "I don't recall doing that though I may have seemed to. I have certainly visited this street before."

"Last night," she said.

"True," he agreed. "I came to look at the cottage. Mr. Murchison was kind enough to give me the keys. I've just rented it."

The explanation took away a good deal of her tension. She studied the powerfully built man with relief. "That explains it," she said.

He offered her that charming smile again and she was struck by his eyes. They had a penetrating directness as he studied her. Now he said, "Mr. Murchison suggested that I meet you after I decided about the cottage."

"Of course," she said with a small smile of her own. "Won't you come into the living room, Mr. Eden?"

"Thank you." And he followed her inside.

She took a seat on the end of a divan and indicated a high-backed chair near for him. He quickly took off his raincoat and then sat down. "A nasty day," was his comment.

"I understand the spring here can leave a lot to be desired," she said. "You've been living in Cambridge if I remember rightly."

"Yes. But I know I will like the cottage and the summer should be very nice here."

"I'm sure of that," she said. "What is your business, Mr. Eden?"

He was staring at her to the point of making her uncomfortable. "I'm retired," he said quietly.

"Oh, yes," she said rather flurried, aware of his eyes. "I believe Mr. Murchison did tell me that. We've just rented the house next door to some people from Boston. I believe they also are retired."

"Yes," he said in the same quiet tone.

There was a pause. An awkward one. Then she said, "If I may speak frankly, you seem young for retirement. I mean you must be a long way from sixty-five."

"That's true."

She felt another silence coming up and began to wonder about her visitor. Again she improvised awkwardly, "But I expect people are retiring earlier in this affluent age. At least I'm told it's affluent. Neither of the Harper brothers seems much older than you."

"You have met William and James Harper?"

"Yes."

"And Maria?"

"Yes. I spent some time with them last night as a matter of fact," she said. "They seem very close as a family."

"I expect so," the stocky man said with a veiled expression on his tanned, squarish face. And very abruptly, he asked, "Are you a strong believer in fate, Miss Waters?"

The question came as a surprise. "I don't know. I haven't thought about it."

"You should," Henry Eden said. "I'm a great admirer of Napoleon and he once said, 'Our hour is marked, and no one can claim a moment of life beyond what fate has predestined.' I think that makes sense, don't you?"

Puzzled by this turn in the conversation, she told him, "I don't think I've developed a habit of philosophical thinking. Perhaps I'm too young."

"Young and lovely," he said with his eyes never leaving her. "You should be willing to defer any other attributes for those two qualities. Youth and beauty can fade with cruel swiftness."

"I haven't had to consider that yet," she said, not understanding why he was talking this way. And he was staring at her almost as strangely as the Harpers had. This led her to another thought. When she'd mentioned the Harpers he'd seemed to know them.

His hands moved restlessly on the carved oak arms of the chair in which he sat. Still studying her, he said quietly, "I mentioned fate because I believe it is no accident that I am here today. I'm sure that we were meant to meet."

She frowned slightly. "Why do you say that?"

"I have good reason," he spoke in the same soft, assured manner. And there was something in his tone that set her nerves further on edge.

Groping for something to change the subject, she ventured, "You spoke just now as if you knew the Harpers."

"Yes. I know them."

She felt another silence coming and

staring at him in the murky gray light of the huge living room wondered what sort of man this was. In the distance the foghorn gave its warning.

She said, "Well, I'm happy you've rented the cottage and I hope you'll like it."

"Yes," he said vaguely. And then he stood up. Looking directly down at her, he said, "May I speak to you very frankly, Miss Waters?"

Somewhat taken back, she said, "About what?"

"A matter that should be of particular interest to you, Miss Waters," he said.

"I don't understand."

"You will," he promised. "Though I must ask you to consider what I have to say in the strictest confidence."

Vera's uneasiness increased. She began to wonder if she were dealing with some sort of demented person. There had been the business of his standing across the street spying on her and the house. Now he was indulging in all this sinister talk.

She suggested, "If this is so serious a subject perhaps you should bring it to the attention of John Murchison."

The tanned, square face lost some of its charm to an angry expression. "This is not for your lawyer's ears but for yours."

"Then please explain yourself."

"Do we have complete privacy here?" he demanded.

More dubious about him than ever, she said, "As much as we require. No one is listening to us."

He seemed to want to make sure of this for he abruptly left her and walked to the open double doorway of the shadowed room and glanced into the hall to make certain there were no eavesdroppers out there. And then he went down to the door at the other end of the room and opened and closed it making sure there was no one in that hall either.

Returning to stand before her he said in an urgent voice, "You may think those precautions silly on my part but I can't risk having what I'm about to tell you overheard."

She was convinced he had to be some sort of crackpot and determined to call John as soon as she'd gotten rid of him and insist that he be removed from the cottage in some way. She could not see him as a desirable tenant. But for the moment she was forced to humor him.

"Please go on," she urged him.

"You've met the Harpers," he said, staring at her with grave eyes. "Have they by any chance mentioned that you resembled their dead niece, June Amory?"

The question came as a shock. "Yes," she admitted.

"Yes," he said with a deep sigh. "They would be bound to do that. You see you resemble her so closely, you could be her twin."

"It is a coincidence," she agreed. "But why make so much of it?"

He smiled grimly. "That's a good question. Why, indeed?"

She stared up at the stocky man's tanned, good-looking face. "You haven't answered me."

He raised a hand. "I will. May I ask you another question first?"

"Well?"

"Did the Harpers sign the lease for the house next door before they met you or after?"

She considered. "It was after. At my lawyer's office."

"Yes," he said with that tormenting quiet assurance. "It would be bound to be that way."

"Now please explain what this is all about."

He eyed her in stony silence. Then he said, "It's about murder, Miss Waters. Yes, I'm very much afraid it's about murder!"

She was even more certain now this stocky man looming before her was insane. "Murder!" she gasped.

"Before you jump to any wrong conclusions, Miss Waters, let me explain that I was a private detective up to the time of my retirement. And I still keep my hand in the game every now and then."

Vera listened to him and studied him with fear in her eyes. Yet there was complete conviction and authority in his manner and his words. She no longer had any doubt that he was responsible.

"Tell me more," she said.

Henry Eden rubbed his hands together in a nervous gesture. "The truth is I think you're in grave danger. And I have come here to warn you and try to protect you."

"What sort of danger?"

"In danger of being murdered in the same way June Amory was."

Her eyes widened with new terror at the sound of his quiet words. "The niece of the Harpers who looked like me was murdered? They told me she died in an accident!"

His smile was bitter. "It would be what they'd likely say. Especially since one of them was probably the girl's murderer."

"Oh, no!"

"I'm afraid so, Miss Waters," the stocky

man said in his controlled way. "The killer was never found. Suspicion fell on them. They were the ones who gained by the girl's death. They inherited the Amory fortune that would have gone to her."

"How do you know all these things?" she demanded.

"Because Mrs. Amory, the murdered girl's grandmother, hired me to protect her. It was my misfortune that I failed in my job. So I know all that went on then and what's happened since."

She was studying him incredulously. "You're saying that one or all of the Harpers were responsible for that poor girl's death?"

He nodded. "I think she was killed by one of them and the other two know about it. They've lived together ever since the crime in almost complete isolation."

"I can't believe it!" she protested. But she was beginning to recall the rather odd behavior of the trio, and the way they had stared at her when they first saw her. Her resemblance to their murdered niece seemed to place them in a kind of stunned state.

"You had better believe it for your own good," was the stocky man's warning.

"Why have you come here to tell me this?" she asked.

"Because for twenty years I have shadowed the Harpers determined to one day get the proof against the murderer of June Amory. That is why I have come here."

"Do they know that you are a detective and still after them?"

A look of satisfaction crossed the tanned, squarish face. "Fortunately no. The girl's grandmother was very discreet when she hired me. She managed to keep the fact from the Harpers. And even the police investigation failed to tie me in with the case. All these years the Harpers have been blissfully ignorant of my existence. That is why I must have your promise of silence concerning my mission."

She stared at him with baffled eyes. "But how can you afford to make this a life work?"

"Mrs. Amory left me a substantial trust fund in her will. She died not long after her granddaughter was murdered. But she saw that a sum sufficient to my needs was left me. While the Harpers were aware of the request they believed it to be to a household servant of the old woman's. She left similar bequests to several of them. And she wanted to deceive the Harpers about me since she was positive one of them was the killer."

"It doesn't seem possible you could live on the fringe of their lives all those years and not be suspected."

He smiled. "I have been careful. I would not tell all this to you if I did not believe you could be trusted implicitly."

She faltered, "I want to do the right thing but I can't imagine that those three were party to a murder scheme."

"You had better believe it, Miss Waters," Henry Eden said solemnly. "There is not much people won't do for money. And Mrs. Amory was fabulously wealthy. Her granddaughter, June, became her main interest after she lost her only son and his wife. That son was a half-brother to William and James Harper. When Mrs. Amory hired me first it was for two purposes. One, to try and gather information that the car in which her son and his wife had died had been tampered with. She was of the opinion that one of the Harpers had fixed the brakes so they would fail. Secondly, I was to protect June from being murdered."

"And you failed?"

A change came over the stocky man. He sank back down in the chair with an air of complete dejection. He nodded, "Yes. I failed that lovely young woman who resembled you so much. And that is the cross I have had to bear all these years."

Vera found herself getting caught up in

the fantastic account in spite of herself. "Where and how did the killing take place?"

"In a garden behind an ancient brick house on Beacon Street owned by June Amory's grandmother. In spite of her grandmother's warnings June liked to lead a lively life. She traveled a good deal, had just finished her college training at an exclusive girl's school and saw a lot of her Uncle William and James Harper. They were much younger than her parents had been and actually about her own age. And so was Maria, the new wife of James. It was natural that she see the three of them a good deal."

"William Harper has always been a bachelor?"

"Yes."

"And Mrs. Amory blamed one of the three Harpers for her granddaughter's murder?"

"She did. June Amory went away for a vacation somewhere. Her grandmother wouldn't tell me. She didn't confide everything in me. But she made it plain the girl would not need a detective to guard her for that period. So I took another job for those weeks. Then June returned suddenly and I thought there was a great change in her."

"In what way?"

"Her health seemed to have failed. She

was pale and aloof even with me. And she had always liked me. According to her grandmother she phoned James Harper about a game of tennis for the following morning. That night she left her bedroom to take a midnight stroll alone in the garden and somebody was waiting for her there and bludgeoned her to death."

Her face was drawn as she pictured the moonlit garden and the body stretched out there to be found. In a taut voice, she asked, "Why weren't you there to protect her?"

He raised his hands in a despairing gesture. "My own selfishness and stupidity," he readily admitted. "I thought I was entitled to a night off now that June had returned. I took it and as a result she lost her life."

"So you do blame yourself?"

"Yes," he frowned at the rug. "Had I been at the house I would never have allowed her to go into the garden alone. I can't tell myself anything different. So I have dedicated my life to capturing her killers."

"Why blame the Harpers?"

"As I've told you. They are the most logical suspects. To her dying moment Mrs. Amory was certain one of the trio had been responsible for June's murder."

"Did she have any definite clues?"

He looked at her with those penetrating eyes. "Enough for her to want me to remain with the case until I solved it. And one day I shall."

"So you found out the Harpers were moving down here and you followed them?"

"Yes."

She was watching him closely to see any change of expression. She said, "According to William Harper they have been the victims of an obscene hate campaign. They've received threats on the phone and vindictive letters in the mail."

The man in the chair across from her shook his head. "I don't believe it. That's a story he's cooked up for you to explain their peculiar hermit's mode of living."

"You had nothing to do with such a campaign?" she asked. "For you must despise the Harpers if you believe them to be murderers."

The man sitting there in the shadows of the living room looked grim. "I despise them. I'll not deny that. But I have not harassed them. I've simply gone on attempting to find proof of their guilt and waiting for them, at least one of them, to make a fatal slip."

"And you believe that may happen now?"

CHAPTER SIX

The statement came as a shocking climax to all that had been said before. Vera looked at the stocky man in the chair opposite her and uttered an exclamation of dismay. Then she said, "You can't really believe that?"

He nodded slowly. "I do. Otherwise I wouldn't have come here. I wouldn't have taken you into my confidence in this way. I think you are in grave danger."

She still couldn't accept it. She said, "They didn't come here to seek me out. I'm a stranger to them."

"You were," he corrected her, leaning forward so that the gravity of expression on his strong face was plain even in the shadows. "But they saw you and that was unfortunate. The chances are they wouldn't have made up their minds about the house so soon if they hadn't been struck by your likeness to poor June Amory."

"Why should that influence them?"

"I'd say it influenced only one of them. And that person swung the others to taking the house. You attracted the insane killer of the murdered girl. In you, the killer sees June reincarnated. And this mad person will not rest until you are struck down."

She felt limp with fear. "You're saying that we're dealing with a mad man or woman. And that is the way they will reason. So I may be killed for nothing more than a fantastic obsession."

"That about sums it up," he told her quietly.

She touched a hand to her temple and then let it slide down her cheek as she tried to get some order into the chaos of her thoughts. "You feel that one of the Harpers is the killer. But you don't know which one?"

"I've changed my mind about it several times."

"Do they know which one of them is guilty?"

"They may guess but I believe the killer has kept the secret well. The other two probably have suspicions but are not sure. Or maybe all three were in the conspiracy. They've surely kept to themselves in the long years since the murder."

"So according to you they all present a danger to me?"

"That's right," he said. "I debated whether I should warn you or not. It seemed a little too early in the game. But then I remembered that an error in my judgment cost June her life and I knew that I couldn't take any needless risks with yours."

Vera looked at him thoughtfully. "There is a kind of deep feeling in your voice when you speak of her, the girl who looked like me and was murdered. Aside from your being hired to guard her, were you fond of her?"

He looked down at the carpet. "I think I was in love with her. I never did find out how she felt about me. But I know she regarded me as a friend."

"How awful for you that it happened as it did!"

"Yes."

There was another silence between them. Then she said, "What can I do? Shouldn't I explain to my aunt and leave?"

Henry Eden gave her a look of annoyed astonishment. "If you did that, you'd be breaking your promise of silence to me. And you'd be robbing me of perhaps my only chance to get that guilty person."

"You're suggesting that I remain here to act as a decoy?"

"That's about it."

She frowned. "Have you the right to ask that? Why should I risk my life in this way?"

"I think you'd be wiser to stand your

ground," was his advice. "Even if you race off from here the chances are the killer will trace you and kill you. Now that you are known to exist you'll never be safe. Not with June's face."

"And I can't tell my aunt or John Murchison?"

"No. At least not until I give you permission."

"And when might that be?"

He shrugged. "I wouldn't like to say. If you repeat what I've told you to anyone I'll be forced to consider it as a breach of faith on your part. And I'll not do anything to help protect you. In which case I wouldn't like to bet on your chances of remaining alive."

"You're warning me to keep quiet or risk being killed?"

"That's the hard choice and the truth," he said solemnly.

"I don't know what I'll do," she worried.

Henry Eden rose and stood there looking concerned. "The best thing would be for you to relax and do nothing. Let things happen around you. Be sure that I'm on the alert and I won't allow you to be hurt by anyone."

Her eyes met his. "Did you tell her that?"

Pain showed on the tanned, square face.

"Perhaps. It's not kind of you to bring that up. It won't happen again."

"I wonder," she said, rising.

He put on his black raincoat and started moving toward the door. "I'm counting on you to keep your head and not betray my confidence in you."

She smiled ruefully as she walked along at his side. "I've never been in a situation like this before. I may not be equal to it."

He patted her arm as they hesitated before the front door. "I'm sure that you will. And don't try to avoid the Harpers. That would only make them suspicious."

Vera eyed him with alarm. "You don't expect me to go over there and fraternize with them after what you've revealed?"

"It might be wise," he advised her. "I see it as the only way we can bait the killer."

"With me as the bait?"

"I'm afraid it's our only hope," he said.

"I'll make no rash promises," she said.

He gave her a warm glance. "I'm not worried about you," he said. "You're the one I need to help me in this. Together we can settle the question of who the killer is."

"I know so little about what happened back then," she complained.

"You know enough," he said. "I'll be seeing you again. And as these things keep coming back to me I'll explain them to you."

She opened the door for him to exit in the fog. "I'll count on seeing you again soon."

"The killer's twisted mind may stir up action almost at once," he warned her. "But don't worry. I'll be standing by."

"Have you heard about transmigration?" she asked.

The stocky man hesitated in the doorway with the damp seeping in around him. "Yes, I have," he said. "It's strange you should bring that up. I've been thinking about it. In the killer's eyes you will represent June Amory alive again in your body. Her spirit in charge of your thoughts and actions. How terrifying for the murderer!"

"I don't think that can happen," she said hesitantly. "I can't believe that I'm controlled by an alien spirit."

He smiled bitterly. "Your likeness to June belies your thought. Wear her face with caution; such beauty can bring you danger."

"I know."

"I hope I haven't frightened you too much," he said. "I followed an impulse in telling you. And my instincts rarely lead me astray."

"You must meet my Aunt Samantha," she said.

"I'd enjoy it," he told her.

"I hope you can tell her what you've told me at an early date."

He put on his battered felt hat and his resemblance to the figure she'd seen spying on her was complete. Giving her a final glance, he said, "Silence is the key word." And he walked down the steps to disappear in the fog.

She stared after him as he retreated across the street to the cottage in the swirling gray mist. Then with a preoccupied look on her pretty face she slowly closed the door. She leaned against it for a moment striving to control herself now that she was left alone with this shattering revelation.

It had been the strangest conversation she'd ever taken part in. And with Henry Eden gone she found herself wondering if she mightn't have dreamt it all. But she knew this was merely wistful thinking. The retired private detective had been there and had warned her. She was haunted by the grave intensity of his tanned, manly face.

For twenty years he'd watched and waited for one of the Harpers to make a betraying move. Never doubting that one day he'd be able to even the score by proving the guilt of the killer. His utter dedication seemed to indicate that he must have truly loved her murdered look-alike. And it had been an incredible accomplishment for him to keep his identity unknown to the Harpers the entire time. To them he would merely be the new tenant in the cottage across the street.

But she knew better. And she hoped that she would be able to play the part in which he'd cast her. He had risked everything in telling her the truth. The least she could do was try to force some sort of resignation on herself. Be willing to bait the murderer and keep silent to the others. This last was the more difficult. She would feel much better about it if she could only let her Aunt Samantha or John Murchison know what she had learned. But that couldn't be.

Her reverie in the dark reception hall was broken by the phone ringing with a harsh irreverence for her jangled nerves. With a slight start she pulled herself together and went over and picked up the impatient instrument. It was John Murchison on the other end of the line.

"I've been trying to get a free moment to call you," he said. "But I've been especially busy here in the office."

"I'm glad to hear from you," she said sincerely.

The voice at the other end of the line

showed concern. "You sound upset. Anything wrong?"

"No. The phone rang at the moment when I wasn't expecting it."

"There's an actual tremor in your voice," John said. "Did I bring you racing downstairs?"

"It's all right."

"I wanted to tell you I've completed the arrangements for renting the cottage."

"I know," she said. "Mr. Eden has been here to call on me."

"Already?" John sounded surprised.

"Yes. In fact he only left a few minutes ago."

"I told him to drop in on you," the young lawyer said, "but I hardly expected he'd get around to it that soon. Interesting man, isn't he?"

"Very," she said, wondering how much John knew about him.

"I like him," John went on. "Maybe he'll make a nice balance for the Harpers. I'd expect he'd turn out to be a much more pleasant neighbor. He's an interesting conversationalist."

"I noticed that."

John sounded vaguely uneasy. "I have some further information about the Harpers," he said. "I'd like to talk to you about them. I have a town meeting early in the evening. But suppose I come by for you around nine-thirty. We can drive to some roadside restaurant and talk over a snack."

"It sounds like a good idea," she agreed. In her tense mood just being with the pleasant young lawyer would help. She'd be forced to settle for the comfort of his company since she couldn't tell him anything.

"Fine," he said. "Be ready at nine-thirty and I'll drive by for you."

She put down the phone with the prospect of meeting John later in the evening making her feel a little easier. He had been quick to notice her tense state and this worried her. If she betrayed her feelings to this extent the others would soon grow suspicious that she was concealing something. And this could wreck Henry Eden's hopes of trapping the murderer of June Amory.

Making her way up the shadowed stairs she found herself wondering about many things. There were so many threads of the story concerning the murder of twenty years ago with which she was not familiar. If only she knew more about the facts, it would be less difficult for her to understand the macabre situation into which she'd been plunged.

In her bedroom she switched on the light

and went across to the dresser to stare at her even blond features in the mirror. It was a weird feeling to know that she wore the mask of the dead girl. That the face which she had always taken for granted as personal and unique to her should merely be a replica of the features of the wealthy beauty murdered twenty years ago.

A murder that had happened when she was a mere child. The theory of transmigration crossed her mind again and she frowned at her image in the mirror. Had the lost spirit of June Amory somehow found its way to her body and taken possession of it? She had no doubt that was what her Aunt Samantha or any of the others who believed in spiritualism would insist. But she could not accept the idea.

It seemed much more likely that a chance resemblance to the murdered girl was the explanation. The likeness might not even be all that exact. But faded photographs and memories played tricks with the truth. So it was quite possible the murderer of June Amory might look at her and see a remarkable similarity of appearance that wasn't really there.

She gave a tiny shudder and turned from the mirror. The forbidding atmosphere of the bedroom seemed to suddenly press in on her. And she began to have qualms about remaining in it. Could there be some sort of curse, some remnant of that ancient evil lingering in the room? And had it anything to do with her present plight? In her absorption with the murder of June Amory, she had temporarily forgotten about the other murder and suicide which had taken place in the Colonial house next door. The girl in the case had left this room to go to her death in the other house.

She walked over to the window and drawing back the curtain peered out into the foggy darkness. And she saw that there was a light on in the murder room. It gave her an eerie feeling. The blind had not been drawn at the other window and a dark clad figure walked by. She saw the figure at the window for only a fleeting moment but she was sure that it was William Harper. He had apparently chosen the murder room for himself.

Drawing back from the window she considered this. It would have been more likely for Maria Harper to select this room. It was she who had shown the most interest in the legend of the haunted Colonial house. She was the one who had brought the trio to Portland in the first place. Yet the room was being occupied by William. It would have been more convenient for Maria's research into the phantom world for her to have taken it for her own use.

John had mentioned that he'd discovered some new information about the Harpers. It would be interesting to hear just what he'd learned. She doubted that it was anything like the full truth. But he must have found out something. Her insistence that he check on their past had produced some results. She could barely wait to hear what they were.

In this confused state of mind she changed for dinner. It was completely dark by the time she went downstairs and found her Aunt Samantha waiting for her in the living room in her wheelchair. The old woman was in conversation with Mrs. Gaskell when Vera entered the dimly lit elegant room.

The stern face of Aunt Samantha showed an impatient look. "I thought you'd never get down here."

"I was late changing," Vera said. "I had a visitor and he kept me late going upstairs."

"So I understand from Mrs. Gaskell," Aunt Samantha said. And turning to the housekeeper she told her, "Pour my niece a sherry as well." She already had a glass of the ruby liquid in her own hand.

Vera stood by as the sullen Mrs. Gaskell

poured a glass of the wine and handed it to her. She took a sip of it and said, "This is pleasant on such a damp, foggy night."

Her aunt frowned. "You'll see a lot more of them before summer comes. I think I warned you about that. Who was your visitor?"

Vera sat down near her aunt as the housekeeper left them alone. She said, "It was a Henry Eden. John rented the cottage to him."

"Already. I thought he was just negotiating for it."

She stared at her glass. "He appears to have made up his mind quickly."

"He must have. What is he like?"

"I'd call him interesting," she said. "He's retired and used to live in Cambridge. He has traveled a good deal."

The old woman in the wheelchair asked, "Does he have a wife?"

"No. He lives alone."

"What made him decide to come to Portland?"

She hesitated. "I don't really know. Perhaps to get away from the city heat."

"He won't be bothered by that too much here," Aunt Samantha agreed. "Did he tell you any more about himself?"

Vera was startled at the questioning given her by the old woman. And she began to wonder if Mrs. Gaskell had been eavesdropping and reported any of the conversation between her and Henry Eden to Samantha. She hoped not and didn't think it likely. Yet the old woman was insistent in her prying.

"He said very little about himself," Vera told her. "Most of his talk was of a general nature."

Aunt Samantha scowled. "He was here long enough."

"I know."

"You should have been able to get more information about him in that time," the old woman grumbled. "You have a good deal to learn."

She smiled thinly. "I'm not an expert on third degree questioning."

"No one expects you to be. But I like to know the sort of people John is renting my property to. This Eden man will be our neighbor and it is important to know the kind of person he is."

"I'll be seeing John later," she said. "He's coming by for me after nine. Perhaps he'll have something to tell me then."

"I certainly hope so," the woman in the wheelchair said clutching her wine glass in a clawlike hand. "I don't know why but I have the feeling that you're not telling me all that you know."

"I'm sorry."

"It's probably only frustration on my part," Aunt Samantha said shortly. "No need for you to apologize. But I'd like to meet this Henry Eden myself before too long."

"I mentioned that to him and he said he'd enjoy meeting you."

The stern old face showed scorn. "I doubt if he'd find it such a treat. But it should be a good idea. You can let me know when."

"I think you should get to know the Harpers also," Vera ventured.

Her aunt turned obstinate again. "In my own good time," she said. "That woman who is interested in spiritualism would probably plague me if I gave her any encouragement. I prefer not to be bothered."

"But wouldn't you enjoy comparing notes with her? Together you might come up with some new discoveries."

"Not likely," the woman in the wheelchair said. "The danger is that she will destroy the atmosphere for contacting the spirits. It doesn't take much."

"Surely not if she knows what she is doing," Vera said.

"But does she?" the old woman asked. "I'm too old and weary to want to expose myself to finding out." She paused. "By the way that name June turned up on the Ouija board again last night."

"Did it?" Vera asked in a small voice. In the distance the foghorn kept up its monotonous chant.

"Yes. It must mean something," Aunt Samantha said firmly. "You're sure you know no one by that name?"

"Yes, I'm sure."

"There is a June trying to get through to me with some sort of message," the old woman worried. "I'm going to try again tonight."

"How can you be so sure someone is trying to reach you from the other side?"

Aunt Samantha stared at her indignantly. "I can feel the presence," she said. "I always know when the spirits are close."

Vera was left with an awed feeling. Certainly the old woman had the murdered girl's first name right either by accident or through a true example of spirit contact. Would she go on to discover other facts? And if the spirit of the murdered girl was so strongly present was it present in her?

A moment of silence gave way to the distant foghorn's warning again and Vera said, "Shouldn't the dead be allowed to rest? Assuming that they can be reached in a seance."

Aunt Samantha looked grim. "They only

try to get through when they have something important to tell. Often they merely want to offer words of comfort. But then again they may wish to rid themselves of dark secrets, or seek revenge."

She tried to accept this casually, saying, "In other words they don't try to reach earthlings unless they have something important to say."

"Exactly," the old woman in the wheelchair snapped. "Unlike most of the earthlings who chatter incessantly whether they have anything to say or not! Let us go in to dinner!"

So the brief discussion ended between them. Aunt Samantha said little at the dinner table and Vera lost herself in her thoughts. She felt she had managed to give a fair account of herself in concealing what Henry Eden had told her. But her aunt had probed deeply in an effort to get more facts from her. She still wasn't sure whether or not the old woman had been posted on the conversation by the sullen Mrs. Gaskell. But she preferred to think that she hadn't.

When dinner ended Aunt Samantha almost immediately took the stairway elevator to the second floor leaving her alone. She had time to fill in before John would arrive so went to the study in the rear of the house and played some of the fine recordings on the stereo. She sat down to listen to the music. But she did not achieve a full enjoyment of the majestic symphonies. Her mind was still filled with the eerie tale told her by Henry Eden and the terrifying situation in which she found herself.

She left the study with the music still playing and walked along the dark hallway to the front of the house with the sound of a mournful theme fading into the background. Moving to one of the front windows, she stared at the cottage across the street and saw that its windows were lighted but its blinds drawn. She wondered if Henry Eden was at home or whether he was out somewhere in the foggy night. Perhaps watching the Colonial house in which the Harpers had taken residence as he'd been doing on those other nights when she saw him.

Straining her eyes she tried to spot his solitary figure in the shadows of the opposite sidewalk. But she couldn't see anyone. She moved away from the window thinking about him. One thing was certain; he had a hypnotic way of creating assurance and confidence. Though she'd met him only briefly, she felt she could depend on him to protect her to the best of his ability and she also was confident his account of the crime of twenty years ago had been a truthful one.

On the other hand the Harpers had bothered her from the start. The gaunt trio had given her an uneasy feeling when she'd first met them. The hint of evil about them had been real for her. She'd sensed something wrong even before she'd learned of the murder and that one of them was undoubtedly a killer. Now that she was in possession of more facts she knew that her instincts had not betrayed her. The Harpers were a sinister group.

She forced herself to sit down with the evening paper. But though she skimmed over the words she took in little of what she read. After what seemed an unendurable wait, it was time to put on her raincoat and kerchief and stand by the door for John Murchison to come by for her in his car. Not until she tied the kerchief under her chin did she realize she was trembling slightly. The suspense was taking its toll from her. And only a few hours had passed since Henry Eden had talked with her.

The fog was still heavy. She watched from the window by the front door until she finally saw the headlights of a car turn into the street. The thick mist gave the headlights a yellowish, floating appearance as the car came up the street. She drew a sigh of relief and opened the door and went outside. By the time the car halted before the house she had gone down the steps and was standing on the sidewalk.

It was only then that she realized it wasn't John's car and neither was it he behind the wheel. The driver leaned over and lowered the window and she saw it was a much older man than John.

"I seem to be lost," he said. "Is this Essex Street?"

"No," she told him. "I think that is two streets below here."

The man thanked her, adding, "A dreadful night."

"It is," she agreed.

He closed the window and turned the car around. She watched its red tail lights vanish in the heavy mist. The car reached the intersection and its brake lights came on. Then it turned and went down in the direction she had told the driver.

She thrust her hands in her raincoat pockets and hunched her shoulders against the damp chill. It was a miserable night. Since she expected John to arrive at any moment she decided against going back into the house. Instead she began to slowly walk along the pavement. The lights in the cottage were still on and there were some lights in the Colonial house occupied by the Harpers also.

Glancing at the rambling Tudor house in which she was staying with her aunt, she saw that there was a light in Samantha's bedroom. An eerie sensation went through her at the picture of the old woman up there with her Ouija board attempting to contact some voice from the other world. Little did the old woman know what the name June meant in this bizarre situation.

She saw a car approaching up the other street and hesitated between the Colonial house and her aunt's waiting for it to turn the corner. But it didn't. After a moment's hesitation it went on. She shivered from a feeling of fear as well as against the cold. What was keeping John?

The street was dark in spite of the subdued light from the windows of the several houses and she felt she should not be standing there. Henry Eden had cautioned her not to take needless risks and this could certainly be considered one. Yet it was past time for John to arrive and he couldn't be much longer.

She gave a deep sigh and fixed her eyes on the corner where any cars had to turn into the street. She was about to give up and return to the house when she saw a car approaching the intersection at quite a speed and then bear down the street toward her. She felt a sense of relief knowing it must be John.

At the same instant she heard a footstep behind her. And before she could wheel around to see who it was she was seized by unseen hands and literally hurled forward directly in the path of the approaching car. She gave a scream of fear and raised her hands to protect herself against the glare of headlights and the screeching of brakes as she struck the asphalt and blacked out!

CHAPTER SEVEN

The shocked face of John Murchison was staring down at her highlighted in the beam of the headlights. She stirred a little, becoming aware she was still on the roadway where she'd been hurled. Seeing that she was conscious John gathered her up in his arms and brought her to a sitting position.

"Are you hurt?" he asked anxiously.

She looked at him dully. "I don't think so."

"Somehow I stopped the car before it hit you," he said in a tense voice. "You came directly in front of me. Why?"

"Someone pushed me!"

"Pushed you?" he sounded incredulous.

"I'm well enough to stand up now," she said, and allowed him to help her to her feet. She felt no particular pain other than a bruised left elbow. And now she checked to see the condition of her clothes. Her coat had a little wet dirt on it from the asphalt but less than she might have expected. And her stockings didn't seem to be torn. She brushed her coat lightly deciding she'd fared remarkably well in the fall.

He said, "Do you want to go back inside?"

She glanced toward her aunt's house apprehensively. "No," she said turning to him again with a troubled expression on her attractive face. "They apparently didn't hear your brakes when you stopped. If I go in now it will only cause a commotion and lead to a lot of questioning."

The young lawyer studied her worriedly. "You're sure you're all right?"

"Yes. My clothes aren't dirtied or torn."

"It's a miracle they're not," he told her. "If you're sure you feel well enough, we can be on our way. But first what's this business about your being pushed?"

"That's what happened. I didn't walk in front of your car. Someone shoved me."

He looked about him in the quiet, fog-ridden street. "Who?"

"I can't tell you that. I didn't see who it was. It could have been anyone."

John was angry. "It had to be a maniac to pull a trick like that. It's just luck that you weren't killed or badly injured."

She looked at him grimly. "I know that. But it will do no good to make a fuss about it. Whoever did it is a long way from here now or has a neat alibi."

"Didn't you hear or see anyone before it happened?"

"I heard a footstep. But before I could find out who it was I was hurled forward."

The young lawyer frowned. "Perhaps we should check with the Harpers and that other new man across the street. They may have seen something."

"If they had they would have heard the screech of your brakes. And no one has come out." She looked in the direction of the Colonial house and saw that all the windows were dark now. "Anyway there doesn't seem to be anyone up at the Harpers."

He gave the Colonial house a hasty glance and then looked over at the lighted windows of the cottage. "He must be awake over there."

"I don't think he's even in the house," she said. "His car is gone. He's just left the lights on."

John was reluctant to go without making some inquiries. He suggested, "Perhaps someone at your aunt's saw or heard something?"

"I'm sure they didn't," she said hurriedly. "Let's go. I could do with some hot coffee. My head is beginning to ache."

He helped her into the car and then drove to the nearest roadside eating place at that end of the town. When they were comfortably installed at a table in the almost deserted big restaurant, he gave her an odd look.

"I don't understand it," he said. "I mean the way you acted back there. You seemed afraid to make any fuss. You acted as if you wanted to gloss the whole thing over!"

She took a sip of her hot coffee and knew she had to handle this situation very carefully. She had to let him understand she was in danger without telling him all the details.

"I didn't want to create a lot of excitement because I was sure it wouldn't accomplish anything," she said.

He was scowling. "Someone tried to kill you."

"I don't know what they intended to do," she sighed. "But they certainly meant me no good. Yet how are you going to prove who it was? I didn't see anyone. It happened in the open street so it could have been anyone. I was foolish to stand out there waiting for you."

"Why did you do that?"

She explained to him about the first car and her thinking it had been he. She ended with, "We can assume there is some malicious person or someone definitely insane at large in the area."

"Why pick on you?" he grumbled.

"Because I made the mistake of standing out there in the dark alone." It was hard not to tell him what she really believed. That it was the murderous one of the Harper trio who had stalked her out there in the foggy blackness and tried to eliminate her.

"The police should be told," John said.

"I doubt if they'd be able to help."

"At least they could have one of their patrol cars keep an eye on the area," the young lawyer said.

"Tell them if you like," she said. "I doubt if whoever it was will come back." At the same time she was wondering where Henry Eden had been when the attack was made on her. She supposed she couldn't expect him to be everywhere but he had promised to protect her. And this time he'd failed badly.

"I'll give them the full details of the incident," he promised.

She stared across the table at him in the soft lighting of the large room. "Just don't have them coming around asking a lot of questions. That would be bound to upset Aunt Samantha and I don't want that."

He took a deep breath. "I must say you don't seem too upset about it."

She made a tiny futile gesture with her

right hand. "It happened and there's nothing we can do about it. I'll be more careful in the future."

"At least I hope you've learned that lesson," he said.

She gave him a wan smile. "Let's not dwell on it any longer. I looked forward to this evening with you. Now it's being spoiled."

Her frank appeal helped lift him out of his concerned mood a little. He sat back in his chair. "I'm sorry," he said. "I wanted this to be a good evening too."

"So let's make the best of it."

The young lawyer studied her with a puzzled look on his pleasant face. "You're a strange girl," he said. "I can't always follow your moods."

"Better not to try," she advised with another smile.

"I'm beginning to think that," he said. "How did you get along with the new tenant for the cottage?"

"Very well."

"I thought you would. He impressed me as a solid type."

"A whole lot nicer than any of the Harpers."

John smiled sheepishly. "You haven't changed your mind about them?"

"I'm not likely to," she said. "From the beginning they've seemed a strange group.

Didn't you say on the phone you'd found out something about them?"

"Yes. I did make some inquiries about them chiefly because you were so insistent that I should."

"And what did you find out?"

He hesitated in answering her and glanced down the length of the nearly empty restaurant. There were a few people seated on stools at the bar and perhaps a half-dozen of the tables were occupied. Muzak played in the background and their waiter stood a distance away surveying them and the array of empty tables around them with a bored look on his puffy face.

After he'd taken this all in John turned to her and said, "What I found out isn't all that important."

"I'm waiting to hear," she said.

He frowned. "I'm afraid if I tell you that imagination of yours will snap into action and you'll be thinking all sorts of crazy things."

"Just now you accused me of taking what happened tonight too calmly," she reminded him with a teasing gleam in her eyes. "Just how do you want me to react?"

"In a normal way if that's not asking too much," he said. "No extremes in either direction."

"I'll think about it," she promised.

He gave her a resigned glance. "I received this information from the bank in Boston they've used," he said. "It's very hush-hush and I'm not supposed to repeat it."

"Go on," she ordered him, feeling sure she knew what he was about to tell her.

"This is nothing to panic about," he warned her. "But a long while ago the Harpers were mixed up in a murder investigation."

"You see!"

He raised a protesting hand. "Now wait until I finish. They weren't under suspicion in any way. But they were questioned. It was a nasty business. A niece of theirs was murdered brutally and the killer never has been found. Not long after they inherited a lot of money from the girl's grandmother. One of the Boston papers wrote a story bringing up the murder case again and putting the Harpers in a nasty light. The account suggested they might have been more helpful at the investigation. The result of this was that the Harpers have shunned publicity ever since. That's why they behave so furtively."

She raised her eyebrows. "Well, I'm glad to have some reasonable explanation for their behavior."

"No one has ever accused them of being

involved in the murder," John Murchison said. "The story was a slanted one and I feel sympathy for them. I guess this girl that was murdered was probably the one you resemble. That's why they behaved so oddly when they met you. Your face could only bring up unpleasant memories for them."

"I'm beginning to recognize that," she said grimly.

"So that's all there is to tell," he said. "The Harpers want to keep out of the public eye in case some shady reporter decides to revive all the old scandal about the unsolved murder."

"I don't see why they're so touchy about it if they are not guilty," was her comment.

"You would if you'd look at it in a fair light," he said. "People of their type hate the whisper of scandal. You can imagine how distasteful the experience has been for them."

"You're saying they're overly-sensitive," she suggested with a hint of sarcasm.

He missed the irony of her tone. "I suppose so," he agreed.

"They still make me feel uncomfortable," she said. "I confess your information hasn't made me more sympathetic toward them."

"At least you can try to understand their oddness."

"I'll reserve an opinion on that," she said. And she glanced at her wristwatch. "It's getting late," she said. "I'd better go home."

John seemed to be brooding as he drove her back to her aunt's place. She sat quietly beside him, now and then staring out at the mist-shrouded streets. The occasional pedestrians they passed hurried along the wet sidewalks like phantom figures. Lights from store windows and houses had a blurred yellowish tinge and the overhead street lamps glowed faintly as if they might have been the ancient gas type she'd somewhere read about.

At last they turned into the short dead-end street of houses dominated by Aunt Samantha's rambling Tudor mansion. The lights in the house occupied by the Harpers were all out and only the front door light showed at her aunt's. She glanced quickly across the street and saw that there was a light showing in one of the front rooms of the cottage and Henry Eden's car was now parked in the driveway so she knew he must have returned home.

John brought the car to a halt and glanced across at her. "I'm going to talk to the police directly after I leave here."

"Please handle it with tact," she begged.

"I believe I'm capable of that," the young

lawyer said stiffly. "This is for your good. I don't want a repetition of what went on here earlier tonight."

"I know."

"You must take care from now on."

"I will," she promised wearily.

He leaned closer to her and took her in his arms. "You must have guessed by now that I'm in love with you," he said.

She smiled at him faintly. "I hoped that you were."

"I am," he said. "And nothing must happen to you." He drew her close and gave her a lasting kiss. It was a pleasant ending to a night that had begun in an inauspicious manner. She enjoyed his embrace and was sorry when it was time for them to part.

He saw her safely inside and paused to kiss her briefly again. Then he left, after promising to call her in the morning and advise what the police had to say about the attack on her.

She lingered in the near darkness of the hallway until he had turned the car and driven off into the fog-ridden night. When she saw the red tail lights turn the corner and vanish she was ready to go upstairs. But before doing this she glanced at the cottage across the street just in time to see the single light go out leaving the place in darkness. She could only assume that Henry Eden might have been watching her arrive home in the car from behind his blinds and when he saw her safely inside he had decided to retire for the night.

Mounting the carpeted stairway to the shadowed upper floor she let her hand run lightly along the oak bannister. She moved slowly absorbed in her thoughts, a puzzled expression on her attractive face. Just now John Murchison had openly declared his love for her for the first time. Her thoughts should have been of him and this new happiness in her life. But instead she was thinking of Henry Eden and the tragedy he'd known. The unsolved murder was more prominent in her mind than the remembrance of John's kiss.

She could hardly wait to see the retired private detective and tell him of her near brush with death earlier in the evening. She had no doubt one of the Harpers was responsible. But she'd not been able to tell John that. At least the young lawyer did know about the murder of June Amory though he had no suspicion of the Harpers as being guilty of the crime. And she couldn't advise him of the facts Henry Eden had given her.

Once again she entered the bedroom with its cold, brooding atmosphere. And once again she faced a night of uneasy sleep and nightmares. This time she was pursued by one of the darkly clad Harpers. But in her wild dream she was not able to tell which of the gaunt trio was trying to kill her. The dream went on endlessly and somehow her Aunt Samantha seemed to be mixed up in it. She awoke in the morning with a vivid memory of it all. It was another gray, foggy day.

Soon after breakfast Aunt Samantha came downstairs. Vera was surprised to see the old woman so early in the day. She went to the bottom of the stairway and helped her transfer her crippled body to the wheelchair waiting there.

The old woman settled back with a sigh of relief. "I'm glad that's over," she said. "During this damp weather I have twice the pain."

Vera looked toward the windows and the mist beyond and with a dejected smile told her, "The weather doesn't seem to be improving."

"It won't for a good while," Aunt Samantha declared. "Oh, we may get an occasional fine spell but it won't last until summer is really on the way." She gave her a sharp look. "You were late getting in last night."

"John didn't get here until nearly ten. He had a town meeting."

"So that was it," the old woman said. "Did you have a pleasant time?"

"Very. We had something to eat and drink. And we talked."

The lined, leathery face registered approval. "I'm glad you're getting along well," she said. "He's a fine young man."

"I agree," Vera said.

Aunt Samantha looked secretly pleased. In a gloating tone she said, "My own evening wasn't without interest."

"Oh?"

The old woman leaned forward in the wheelchair. "I spent nearly three hours over the Ouija board. And the spirits had some startling things to tell me."

Vera hardly knew what to say. She had no confidence in the old woman's Ouija board revelations. And yet she had managed to come up with the name June and the date of the murder. Perhaps it wasn't as ridiculous a pursuit as one might think.

So she ventured, "What did it tell you this time?"

The old woman smiled bleakly. "It spelled out a name. But I'll not mention it just yet."

"You have a reason for keeping the name a secret?" Vera questioned her, wondering what was behind the mysterious front the old woman was offering.

"I do," Aunt Samantha said firmly. "About that caller you had yesterday."

"Mr. Eden?"

"Yes. The new tenant in the cottage. Didn't you say he was anxious to meet me?"

"He said he'd enjoy it."

"Well, I'd like to know him," the old woman said. "You can tell him he can come over to dinner tonight."

"I'll be glad to," Vera said. "Though it is short notice and I don't know whether he'll be able to come or not."

"He'll come," Aunt Samantha said firmly. "Few people ever refuse my dinner invitations. I'd like to hear his impressions of Portland. It's not often I see a new face. It should do me good."

So it was settled as far as the old woman was concerned. Vera promised to go over and invite Henry Eden for the evening meal. In the meantime Aunt Samantha went off to the kitchen at the rear of the house to discuss the menu for dinner with the cook. She propelled herself down the dark hall in her wheelchair with an astonishing swiftness.

She'd barely vanished when the phone

rang. And when Vera took the call she was surprised to find that it was the younger Harper brother, James, on the line.

"Miss Waters?" he asked in an irritated tone.

"Yes," she said, wondering what was wrong.

"I'm sorry to tell you we were bothered last night," James Harper declared.

Vera felt the conversation was beginning in an unexpected manner. She said, "In what way were you bothered?"

James Harper sounded cold and angry. "In a very familiar way, Miss Waters. Early last evening the phone rang and when my wife answered it she was the target for another of the obscene calls with which we've been plagued."

She listened with some disbelief. "How could anyone know that you'd moved here this soon?"

"I can't tell you that," the younger Harper brother snapped. "I can only say that we're all upset about it."

"I'm sorry," she said.

"It may be that we'll not be able to remain here after all," James Harper went on. "If this torment is to begin again I, for one, am not ready to face it."

"Perhaps it was only a coincidence," she

suggested. "It may have been someone else. Obscene calls are unfortunately not confined to any one city."

"This was the same person who called us continually in Boston," he said. "Maria recognized his voice. And the tenor of what he said was the same as in the past."

Vera said, "I suggest you call John Murchison. He may have something helpful to offer."

"I'm going to," James Harper said. "In fact I think my brother and I will go down and see him. We will have to discuss the possibility of our not staying in Portland."

"I hope it's not all as bad as that," she said.

"It is bad enough," James Harper said. "I wanted you to know before I saw your lawyer."

"Thank you," she said. "I'll be interested in hearing what he has to suggest."

"I'll be in touch with you later," James Harper promised and he hung up.

She put down the phone with a frown. And at once she decided to try and reach John since he'd not already called. She found the number for his office and his elderly female secretary came on the line.

"Who will I tell Mr. Murchison is calling?" she asked.

"Vera Waters," she said. "I won't keep him a moment. It's urgent."

"I'll see," the woman said peevishly.

There was a buzzing on the line and then she heard John say anxiously, "Is that you Vera?"

"Yes."

"Anything wrong?"

"Nothing to worry about. But I felt I should contact you."

"I talked with the police," he said. "They're going to investigate last night but they'll be discreet. It is possible one of the plainclothesmen will come by to question you."

"I hope they are discreet," she said with meaning. "You know how Aunt Samantha is. I'm calling you because James Harper just phoned me."

"About what?"

"They received an ugly phone call last night. Similar to ones they had been getting before they left Boston. He's very bothered and I think he and his brother are going down to see you. They may want to break their lease."

"That's really news!" John said with a small gasp. "I'm glad you warned me. You say they've had these crackpot calls before?"

"Yes."

"Any idea of the nature of them?"

"They didn't go into that. He termed them obscene."

"I see," John said grimly. "Well, at least now I'll be prepared for them."

"I thought you should be," she said. "Perhaps you ought to let them leave if they want to."

"I don't regard leases that lightly," was the young lawyer's reply. "You needn't worry. I think I can manage them."

"Let me know what happens," she told him before she ended the conversation. As soon as she put down the phone she went across to the window and looked to see if Henry Eden's car was still parked in the driveway of the cottage. It was. And so she decided to hurry over and speak to him before he had a chance to get away.

She put on her raincoat and kerchief. They had become a sort of uniform with the bad weather. And as she slipped into rubbers she felt thankful that the Harpers had no idea who Henry Eden was. They wouldn't have any suspicions about her going over to talk with him. She left the house and found the day almost as miserably damp as the night before.

It took her only a moment to cross the street and mount the front steps of the cottage. She rang the doorbell and waited. After a short wait the door was opened to reveal the stocky Henry Eden in his shirt sleeves. He looked slightly embarrassed.

"You've just caught me cleaning up my breakfast dishes, Miss Waters," he said with a smile. "Won't you come in?"

"I'm sorry to intrude," she said. "But I have two urgent things to discuss with you."

He closed the door after her and showed her into the medium-sized, modestly furnished living room. Waving her to an easy chair, he said, "You must never worry about bothering me. I count on your cooperation."

"For one thing," she said, as she sat, "my aunt wants you to join us for dinner at seven."

"I'll be glad to," he said, hurriedly putting on his suit jacket. He stood in the center of the room then, waiting to hear whatever else she might have to tell him.

"And something unpleasant happened to me last night," she said. And she told him about being shoved in front of John's car.

He listened with a frown on his tanned, square face. She noticed in this better light that his black hair was thinning. He said, "I'm not surprised they made their first attempt on your life. I'm only shocked that I happened to be in downtown Portland at the time."

"You wouldn't expect me to be standing out there in the dark alone."

"Frankly, I wouldn't," Henry Eden said solemnly. "You took a fantastic chance and the killer almost got you. It should be a lesson to you."

"It will," she said contritely.

He sighed. "That doesn't make me feel any better for not being there. I'll try to be on hand when the next attack comes."

She looked at him with fear in her eyes. "You seem very sure there will be another one."

"It's bound to happen," he said definitely. "The sick mind of the murderer makes that certain. In you he sees June Amory."

"I'm not sure the Harpers will remain here," she informed him. And then she went on to tell him about the phone call she'd received from James Harper.

When Henry Eden had heard the details he smiled wisely. "Surely you can see through that move?"

"I'm afraid not."

"It's too obvious," the stocky man said with a grim note in his voice. "They wanted to take the offensive. To accuse somebody else of bothering them so you wouldn't dream of thinking one of them had attacked you. It's a stunt to throw you off guard."

"I suppose it could be," she marveled.

"The Harpers are wily ones. And perhaps James Harper is the most astute of the three."

"You think they never received the obscene call?"

"I do."

She saw that he was probably right. The Harpers were shrewd. And at least one of them was a killer. She must always be skeptical of anything they might say.

She gave him a questioning look. "What next?"

"I have plans," he said with that strange assurance. "But first I want to show you something." And he reached into the left pocket of his jacket and drew out a small gold locket with a thin chain. "This is a locket that once belonged to June Amory's grandmother. She gave it to me shortly before she died. The last time I saw her."

Vera eyed the locket. "It's lovely."

"And it has a special interest for me and I think for you," the stocky man said as he carefully opened it to reveal a snapshot in one side of it and a coiled lock of blond hair in the other. He held the locket close against

CHAPTER EIGHT

Vera stared at the twist of hair in the locket with a fascinated revulsion. The retired detective was right. The hair, even after all these years in the locket, matched hers very well in color and quality. It was hard to believe that the girl from whose head this hair had been cut had some twenty years before been bludgeoned to death.

"It is like my hair," she said in a small voice.

"I wanted you to see it," the stocky man said, still holding the locket close to her.

"I can't visualize her dead so long," Vera spoke with awe.

"I know what you mean," Henry Eden said in a tone rich with understanding. He drew the locket away from her and snapping it shut put it back into his pocket. "I suppose I shouldn't have let you see that. It's a grisly souvenir. But I hoped it would do you some good."

Her eyes widened. "In what way?"

His glance was solemn. "I wanted this to be an object lesson. To make you understand this was a living, laughing, wonderful girl who was murdered, someone a lot like you. And what happened to her could happen to you."

"After last night I don't find it hard to believe."

Henry Eden nodded. "I hate asking you to make a decoy of yourself. And I don't want you taking a lot of foolish risks. But I would like you to remain here until I have finally pinned June's murder on the right Harper."

She met his eyes. "You're still positive it was one of them?"

There was conviction in his returning glance. "More than ever," he said quietly.

"And now this long while later, the murderer is stalking me."

"Yes," Henry Eden said in his soft fashion. "But we shall use that as a trap; wait and see."

"I'll try to do as you suggest," she said.

He was wearing a gray tweed suit that gave him the air of a man of authority. She was struck by his neat manner of dressing. He was careful in his choice of clothes and wore things that suited him. He was putting on some extra weight now but she could see that when he was younger he must have been a handsome man. She could understand why the murdered girl's grandmother would have confidence in him and hire him for the delicate task of saving the girl's life.

What puzzled her was that he had failed. He did not seem the type of man who accepted failure lightly. But it was impossible to always predict the behavior of people and that was how he had been caught off guard. Just as he had been last night when she'd chosen to disregard caution and go out on the street in the darkness and wait for John's car. She should never have done such a thing.

The stocky man was moving over to the fireplace now. In front of it he turned with a slight frown on his face. "The one thing you must always keep in mind," he warned her, "is that you are dealing with an insane person."

"I suppose he'd have to be."

"Without a question," he said grimly, his hands clasped behind his back. "And yet a maniac capable of cloaking that madness and showing the public a perfectly normal face."

She shivered. "I find that idea terrifying."

"Be terrified," was his advice. "Fear could save your life."

"If only I dared discuss it with other people," she told him. "If I could warn my aunt or John Murchison it would be so much easier."

He shook his head gravely. "Out of the question. A secret shared is no longer a secret. Our murderer would smell the plot against him at once. I took a calculated risk in telling you. Though I now feel it was one that couldn't be avoided and that will work out."

She smiled wanly. "I know you're right about the silence. Still it's hard."

"Righting such a wrong is bound to be difficult," he said, studying her with serious eyes. "But in the end it will be worth it. And I think it ironical that the identical lovely face that drove our maniac to murder before will make him attempt the same crime again!"

"What do you suppose will happen next?" she wondered.

His smile was grim. "One or another of the Harpers will make some overture to you. Some gesture of friendship and then when you're unsuspecting they'll try to finish you off."

"A bleak prospect. As dismal as the endless foggy days."

The stocky Henry Eden marched over to the window and stared out at the dark, misty day. "I rather like this fog," he said.

"I'm glad. You're apt to see a good deal of it if what everyone says is true."

"I remember a poem about fog," the retired detective said, turning to her, "I think it went 'The ghost am I, Of winds that die, Alike on land or sea.' I don't know the rest of it."

"Fog does make one think of ghosts," she agreed with a sad smile. "You seem a very literate person for someone who admits to having been a private detective."

He mused in a forlorn fashion. "I hope you don't cast all detectives to type as having marble heads and size twelve shoes. Raymond Chandler and Dashiel Hammet notwithstanding many detectives, private and on the regular force, are men with education."

"Of course I understand that," she said. "But I meant something special in your case. I think you're a sensitive person."

Henry Eden looked at her hard and then slowly walked over to her. "I'm glad you said that. Because I believe it is true."

"I'm sure it is."

He wore a far-away look on his tanned, squarish face. "It's also strange that you should make such a comment since June Amory said the same thing to me not long before she was killed."

Vera gave him an incredulous smile. "Not really!"

"Yes," he said with a sigh, his hands still clasped behind his back. "We were talking one day a good deal as we're talking now. Of course no mention had been made of a murder attempt on her. It was part of my agreement with her grandmother that the threat should never be discussed. June knew that she was a possible target for criminals because of her wealth and accepted me as her bodyguard."

"And friend?"

"Close friend, I hope," he said sadly. She could tell by his manner that he was suddenly lost in the past. "We were strolling in the garden. The very garden in which she was murdered. And she spoke to me of my being a sensitive person. I hoped then that she might be seeing me as a man and not just as an employee. And I think that for at least a little time she measured me that way. I like to imagine that a romance would have developed between us if she hadn't been taken from me in that horrible fashion."

She studied him with sympathy. "You've never married?"

"No."

"In a sense you've been true to her. Apparently no other woman has had any interest for you."

"That is so," he said in his quiet way. "I don't think there's any point in my trying to conceal the fact that I loved June. And because of that my mission to capture her killer is more than a debt of honor to her grandmother, or an act of vengeance on my part, it is something about which I have no choice. I must erase the violence of that awful night!"

She saw the veins bulge at his temple, the tiny beads of sweat ooze out there and she pitied him. Of course he had loved June Amory and lived in torture ever since her murder. And now the macabre drama was to be played again if the insane killer reacted as they expected.

She said, "Do you think it was William Harper who did it?"

She'd put the question to him in an effort to bring him out of his unhappy mood. And to a degree it worked. Some of the tension left him and he gave her a troubled glance. "He could have," he said. "In the beginning I was sure he was the guilty one. He was in love with June."

"You're sure of that?"

He smiled bleakly. "Since I loved her myself it wasn't a fact liable to escape me. I knew William was a rival. He was only twenty-five then but even in those days he had that stiff, bachelor's manner about him. He didn't get along with girls easily. And June used to tease him."

"Did she know his feelings toward her?"

"Yes. I gathered from what she let drop to me that he'd actually proposed to her. Her grandmother didn't approve of the idea since she regarded William Harper as family though there was only a scant blood tie between him and June."

"Nothing came of the romance?"

"No. I suppose again it's hard to predict what could have happened if June hadn't been murdered. I had a theory for a while that he'd proposed to her a second time and she'd rejected him and made fun of him. And in a person of his tense, withdrawn nature such a situation could produce a motive for murder."

"But she was killed so brutally. Surely he wouldn't bludgeon her to death in that fashion!"

Henry Eden shrugged. "I wouldn't rule out the possibility. In a moment such as that he would be out of control. In his rage it might give him pleasure to inflict that kind of punishment on her. I gave most of my time to him in the first few months after the murder. I was positive he was the one. But later I began to have other ideas."

"What brought them about?"

"A number of things," he said frowning as he recalled those unhappy days. "I think I told you that just prior to the actual murder June went away from Boston for several weeks."

"I think you did."

"There was a lot of mystery to her going," Henry Eden said in a troubled voice. "Her grandmother had hired me to protect her but she wouldn't hear of my going with June on this trip."

"Where did she go?"

"I never found out," he said. "During the investigation there was a mention of a short visit with a cousin in Syracuse but I'm positive she wasn't there all the time. And that became the basis for my other suspicions."

"Please go on."

"It's not easy to talk about," he sighed. "But I began to believe that June had gone on that trip because she'd not had any choice. In the month before she went she was pale, restless and not like her normal self."

"You think she was ill?"

He nodded grimly. "Yes. I told you that she and James Harper had been seeing a lot of each other even though he'd just married Maria. He and June still were very close. And I think she would have married him if he'd asked her. But he didn't. After his marriage they kept meeting for tennis and other dates. And one day I happened to overhear June and Maria having a quarrel about him."

Vera opened her eyes wide. "It was that bad?"

"Yes. Maria warned June to stop seeing her husband and June refused. But after that she didn't so boldly date her young married cousin. Yet I have an idea they met secretly. And I think it could have been James who made her pregnant so she was forced to have that trip for an abortion."

"You really think that?"

"Yes," Henry Eden's face wore a haunted look. "Now this could have set up a murder motive for either one or two persons. June could have threatened to tell her grandmother who had gotten her pregnant. And James could have made up his mind to murder her to silence her and prevent any threat to his legacy from the old woman or any break-up of his marriage."

"I can see that he would have a motive," she agreed.

"Or it could have been Maria," Henry Eden reminded her solemnly. "Jealousy of her husband and a desire to protect their legacy could have made a strong enough reason. And neither James nor William need to have been accomplices."

"That's true."

"Or on the other hand they might both have been," the detective said with bitter resignation. "So we're back to where we started. Either one or all three of the Harpers murdered her. And either one or all three of them will try to murder you."

"I can see how they fit into this more neatly now," she said. "Thanks for telling me what you have."

"I'm glad to," he said. "After all you're risking your life to help me solve this nasty riddle. As I recall details I'll try and pass them on to you."

"You're carrying a grim burden on your own shoulders," she marveled. "Wouldn't you do better to take the police into your confidence?"

He shook his head. "I've tried that. In the years right after June's murder and it did no good. They labeled my theories as fantastic, put the murder down to an unknown prowler, ignored all the evidence I showed them pointing to the Harpers and asked me not to bother them again. So I haven't."

"I think you're wonderful to have carried

on as you have," she said. "Not many people would do it."

He smiled bleakly. "Give the credit to Grandmother Amory who made me financially independent so I could devote all this time to a lost cause and to June who will always be an inspiration to me."

She was once again touched by the gentleness of his voice. And she knew that he had truly been in love with that other girl who looked like her and for whom he was still mourning. She said, "I must go back and tell Aunt Samantha you've accepted her dinner invitation. She predicted that you would. She says no one ever refuses her."

The detective showed amusement on his square face. "Such assurance shouldn't be shaken. I'll be there at seven. And in the meantime watch yourself."

"I've learned my lesson," she said.

He saw her to the door and as he opened it for her, he said, "May I confess that in the short time I've known you I've become very fond of you?"

She gave him a friendly smile. "I like you, too."

"Thank you," he said. "It's as it should be. It's almost like having June back again. You have no idea how closely you resemble her."

"I've accepted that."

"The likeness is amazing," he said, studying her intently. "I hope that young man of yours, the lawyer, doesn't object to our friendship."

"Of course not," she said. "I haven't been able to tell him much. But I'm sure he'd be happy to know we're friends."

"One of the few advantages of becoming middle-aged," Henry Eden said warmly, "is that one is allowed a platonic friendship with young women. I'll see you and Mrs. Waters promptly at seven."

Embarrassed by his sudden show of emotionalism she quickly bade him goodbye and hurried across to her aunt's place again. It was misting heavily now, so much so that she wondered if it would turn to rain. When she encountered her aunt in the rear parlor she suggested the possibility and Samantha at once refused to take it seriously.

"It won't rain," the old woman in the wheelchair said. "But this ugly fog will continue."

"Henry Eden agreed to join us for dinner," she told Samantha.

"I expected that," her aunt said.

"How could you be so certain?" Vera demanded with amused surprise.

"I can't tell all my secrets," was her aunt's

rather taunting reply.

The day proved to be an uneventful one. At least until shortly after luncheon. Then, when Aunt Samantha had fortunately gone up to her room for a nap, the man from police headquarters arrived to question Vera, Mrs. Gaskell let him in and Vera at once took him to the study where she could close the door without their being overheard.

As soon as she was alone with the plainclothesman, she said, "I asked Mr. Murchison to request that no one come here."

The plainclothesman was tall, lantern-jawed and graying. He gave her a grim eye. "Once he spoke to us there was no question of our calling on you. It's a matter of routine. I'll be in charge of the investigation and I'll keep it as discreet as possible. My name is Inspector Hannigan."

"Thank you, Inspector Hannigan."

"If you ever want to have headquarters help you it would be wise to mention my name," he continued. "Now I'd like to ask you some questions about last night." And he proceeded to do this.

Vera tried to make it brief. At the same time she gave the most honest replies she could without dragging Henry Eden into it.

When she finished she saw that Inspector Hannigan was regarding her with a frown.

"I think I've told you all I can," she said, wondering why he was looking at her in this troubled way.

"You're sure you're not forgetting anything?" he asked. He had a colorless voice.

"I've given you all the details."

He nodded. "Thank you. I sort of have the feeling you may have forgotten something. It's just a hunch. But every fact is important when you realize that your life may be at stake."

She knew she must be careful to protect Henry Eden and the secret they shared. Cautiously, she said, "If I knew anything else I'd surely be quick to tell you."

"I guess you would," he agreed. He was wearing a rumpled gray topcoat and no hat. "There are a few characters in this area we keep an eye on. I'll be questioning some of them. And if anything happens here you get in touch with us."

"I will," she said. "And thank you."

"Our pleasure," he said in his bleak way. And she showed him out.

She was actually relieved to see him drive away. It was good to know the police were there to call on. And she couldn't blame John for what he'd done. He'd simply been doing what he could to protect her. But she had to put them off until they'd lured the murderer into the open. And that wasn't going to be easy.

Henry Eden's car was still in the driveway by the cottage and she wondered if he'd seen the car stop in front of her aunt's place. He would have no way of telling who it was. The car had been a plain one and the inspector hadn't been in uniform. She decided it would be best not to mention that the police had been notified. Let Henry Eden think the caller was some sales person or repair man. If he heard about John contacting the police he'd only be badly upset for no reason. She could handle the situation better on her own.

At least she was beginning to have that much confidence in herself. She had found enough courage to want to see the project through. Gradually she had come to feel an empathy with the dead June Amory. She didn't for a moment believe it was transmigration or any of the spiritualism mumbo-jumbo her Aunt Samantha would probably suggest. She felt it was because she had gotten an insight into what the beauty murdered twenty years ago had been like through Henry Eden. And she was beginning to understand her and the problems she'd faced.

* * *

The phone call from Maria Harper came shortly after two-thirty. Not long after the police inspector had driven away. Vera took the call with some wariness, not able to guess what it might mean.

Maria sounded apologetic, "I hope I didn't disturb you."

"No," she said. "I was just standing looking out at the fog and hoping it might disappear."

"It is a gray day," Maria agreed. "I've phoned you because I'm all alone in the house and a little nervous."

"I'm sorry," she said. She was cautious in her reply because she wondered whether the frail wife of James Harper was telling the truth or whether it was part of some ruse to trap her.

"My husband and his brother have gone down to the real estate office," Maria continued.

Vera knew this was liable to be true since James had mentioned it to her earlier. She said, "No trouble I hope."

"Things aren't turning out well," Maria lamented. And then she said, "I wish you'd come over here for a few minutes. I have some things to tell you I can't say over the phone."

It was a moment for caution. Maria had given her an open invitation to join her in the old house. It could be the warning of a second attempt on her life. But would they dare try anything this risky? She doubted it.

She said, "I might go over for a short time. My aunt is expecting company this evening. I have to help her get ready for it."

"If you'd only come for a brief while it would mean so much to me," the woman at the other end of the line said eagerly.

"I'll be over shortly," she said.

As soon as she put the phone down she went across to the window with the idea of getting in touch with Henry Eden and telling him what she was going to do. But once again the detective's car was not in the driveway. He was away from the cottage. It could be he'd followed the Harpers when they'd left for the business district. In any event it put her in a difficult spot.

She realized that she'd have to go over for a visit with Maria or rouse the frail woman's suspicions. Since neither William nor James Harper was in the house she felt it would be reasonably safe. She'd listened to all Henry Eden's theories as to who the murderer could be among the trio and she'd felt Maria was the least likely suspect.

She barely touched the doorbell of the

Colonial house when the door opened and a grateful Maria eagerly invited her in. The intense, dark woman was wearing a dressing gown of some kind of black satin that made her look more sallow than usual and the black shadows under her eyes were heavier than before. Vera thought she looked ill.

Maria led her into the living room and nervously offered her a chair. Then she sat next to her on the edge of a large, overstuffed easy chair. "I stood by the phone a full ten minutes before I had the courage to call you," she told Vera.

Vera smiled. "You shouldn't have been so hesitant."

"I hated to bother you with my troubles and fears," Maria said, clasping her hands and looking down at the carpet.

"What seems to be the problem?"

Maria glanced up at her with frightened eyes. "It's everything. My husband and his brother are quarreling. And you have no idea how violent their quarrels can be. I sometimes think William hates both James and me. That some day he'll murder us!"

She stared at the woman who'd uttered this shocking statement. "Why do you say that?" she asked quietly. Thinking that perhaps the meeting was a lucky one. That she might gain valuable information from the frail, dark woman.

Maria at once became less upset. In a quieter tone, she said, "I shouldn't have said that. But William does have a bad temper. So does my husband. It's a family trait."

"What do they quarrel about?"

The dark woman's eyes were tortured. "We live too close and hermitlike an existence," she said. "We've lived this way for years, shutting out the world for the most part. It's not healthful. Yet we cling together in our flight from reality."

She furrowed her brow. "Why do you call it a flight from reality?"

"It's what it is," Maria declared with some passion. "It mightn't be so bad if James and I were on our own with William living somewhere else. But while I'm sure he hates us, he clings to us."

"For what reason?"

"We share the same fear of the world and what it might do to us," Maria said. "You would not understand. But we have been harassed by the press and cruel people. And it has started again. We have had two hate calls on the phone since we got here."

"It hardly seems possible," Vera said. "You've been here such a short time."

"Whoever it is hates us enough to follow our every move."

"What did he say on the phone?"

"I don't want to think about it," Maria said, tears brimming in the large black eyes. "As a result of the calls my husband and his brother began to argue about whether we should stay here or not. One word led to another. I knew how it would end."

"And so now they've gone to discuss it with John Murchison?"

"Yes. James wants to move and William is against it."

Vera listened with rising excitement. To her it was an important clue. If William was the one who wanted to remain in the old Colonial house it was likely he was the insane killer. And his reason for wanting to stay was so he could finish the business of murdering her.

She said, "I'm sure Mr. Murchison will be able to reason with them."

Maria gave her another of her frightened looks. "Do you really think so?"

"Yes."

"I hope so," the frail dark woman said, glancing apprehensively about the shadowed living room. "This tragic old house both repels and fascinates me. But before I leave I do want to try some psychic contacts."

Vera said, "I won't be of much help in that."

"But I'm sure you can be," Maria said, staring at her earnestly. "You look so much like my dead niece that I almost expect you to speak to me in her voice. It's amazing."

"Perhaps the resemblance is less than you imagine."

"No," Maria argued, "you're very much like her. And she had a sensitive nature. I'm sure you have as well. The main reason I asked you over here today was to help me conduct a short seance."

Vera shook her head. "No. Really!"

"Please," Maria begged. "If my husband decides to leave I may not have another opportunity. And this house is filled with uneasy spirits."

"I'd only spoil your chances," she protested. "I'm not a believer."

"Stay for company," Maria pleaded. "I do not ask anything else. If the spirits are here I'll slip into a trance state. And I won't mind as long as you are present to see that no harm comes to me. When I go into a trance I'm like an unconscious person."

Vera stood up. "I'd rather not."

"I have everything ready," Maria insisted, now actually taking her by the arm.

She hesitated. "Where do you plan to hold the seance?"

A wise smile crossed the sallow, shadowed face. "Where but in the murder room upstairs? It has to be the best place."

The thought of that room sent a chill through Vera. And the idea of a seance there with only Maria as company was even more terrifying. She had a strong desire to break away from the frail, dark woman and get out of the house. But Maria did not release the hold on her arm.

Vera said uneasily, "I'd rather not."

"But you won't refuse me this small wish," Maria said with a kind of hypnotic effect. And before Vera actually realized what was happening she was slowly mounting the murky stairway with the woman in black, heading for the haunted room.

CHAPTER NINE

The great house was cloaked in a deathly silence. Vera felt almost like someone in a daze as she allowed Maria Harper to guide her to the dark landing and then down the corridor on the left to the murder room. Hesitating at the door of the room she was startled to see that it was almost completely in blackness. Maria had drawn the shades and pulled the drapes closed. In the center of the room was a small table with a dark velvet cloth on it and sitting on the cloth was a large glass crystal.

She gave Maria a glance. "Why the crystal ball?"

The frail woman smiled. "I have different means of contacting the other side. Sometimes I induce a trance and then again I gaze into the crystal and the spirits appear in it."

A chill ran down Vera's spine. Was the woman mad? She said, "I haven't any faith in this. It's my aunt whose support you should seek."

Maria's hand on her arm tightened its pressure. "It is you I need," the other woman said. "You mustn't back out on me now."

They went on into the room. There were plain chairs at opposite sides of the table and Maria seated her in one of the chairs and then sat down in the one across from her.

As Vera became accustomed to the almost dark room she was aware that Maria had shut the door behind them when they entered. She was also fascinated by the fact that the crystal ball seemed magically illuminated in some weird way so that a dull glow from it served to highlight Maria's features in a ghostly fashion, and undoubtedly did the same to her own. Peering down at the crystal she tried to discover the secret of the eerie glowing and decided there must be some kind of tiny bulb concealed in its wooden base.

The sallow, gaunt face of the frail Maria had a phantom quality in the dim light. Her eyes burned brightly as she stared at Vera intoning, "You must not be so skeptical. Spiritualism is an established fact of history and religion. In the Old Testament when the Witch of Endor called up the spirit of the prophet, Samuel, she was acting as a medium. The Greeks talked to the spirits through their oracles. And Tertullian, one of the early Christian fathers, describes the early Christians as having divine revelations in trances."

Fear clamped Vera in the chair as she listened to Maria go on in this weird fanatical manner. Surely this was madness! Henry Eden might not be so wrong after all in including this strange woman among his murder suspects.

"I wish you would give up this experiment," she said.

Maria smiled at her oddly. "Too late now. I can feel myself slipping into the trance state. This room is alive with spirits. One will soon take over. My body will be occupied by some wandering soul of the astral plane and perhaps you'll learn what went on in this room the night of the murder and suicide."

"No," she protested, her hands gripping the edge of the velvet covered table, "I don't want to go on with this!"

"Please!" Maria said in an eerie tone. Her eyes were closed and she had begun to sway slightly from side to side.

"Maria!" She cried out the dark woman's name in a frantic manner. She wanted to jump up from the chair and run from the room but her terror froze her where she was.

The glow from the crystal seemed to soften and change in a subtle manner so that the room was even darker than before.

Maria began to moan at intervals as if she were in some kind of intense pain.

"Please! Listen to me!" Vera begged her.

But her only reply was a continuing moaning on the dark woman's part. Maria seemed to have drifted off into another plane of existence. And the gloomy room had taken on a frightening clammy coldness, as if the dead had actually begun invading it.

"Maria! Say something!"

Her reply was a wild scream from the frail, dark woman. Then Maria raised her arms above her head and began sobbing in a loud fashion. Vera sat clenching the edge of the table as she stared at her in terror. Next the sobbing ended abruptly and Maria slumped down in the straight-backed chair so that it seemed she would almost fall to the floor. She was breathing heavily like a stroke victim. And to all appearances she was no longer conscious.

Afraid for her, Vera leaned forward and called to her loudly, "Maria! What is it?"

There was no reaction from the frail dark woman. No opening of her eyes or any attempt to respond on her part. She remained slumped down in the chair in that abject state.

And then Vera heard the strange rustling

movement from close behind her. And the vision of that woman in the photograph who had been murdered there fifty years earlier flashed across her mind. It was as if the sound and the vision of that lovely face were somehow connected. She was sick with terror not daring to look around or move. Certain that Maria had been successful in her psychic experiment and now standing near them was the materialized spirit of the murdered woman.

Hands from behind her closed on her throat. She reached up in a futile attempt to save herself. But it was no good. Those hands were all powerful and now they were exerting a choking pressure that shut off her breath and made her weak. She tried to utter a cry for help but didn't manage it. She gazed at the unconscious Maria with agonized eyes as she felt her own being drain off into darkness under the cruel pressure of those phantom hands. Mercifully she blacked out.

She was crying gently. And when she opened her eyes she was stretched out on the floor with William Harper bending over her. Apparently he'd thrown back the drapes and lifted the shade for the room was filled with grim daylight which enabled her to see everything clearly. It took her a moment to recall why she was sobbing and be aware of her aching throat.

The angular face of the older Harper brother showed dismay as he stared down at her. "What happened?"

"An evil spirit," she whispered. "Maria called on it and then it began to choke me."

William Harper looked annoyed. "I expected a better explanation than that from you," he said. "I know what's wrong with Maria. She's off in one of her self-induced fits. But it has to be different with you."

"I was choked," she told him, sitting up.

"I see that your throat is red," he agreed, examining it. "I can almost tell where the fingers exerted their pressure. The red is clearly outlined."

She reached up to touch her burning throat. And for the first time she began to try and fit the puzzle together. Studying him with suspicion, she said, "When did you get here?"

"Just a few minutes ago," he said. "At first I thought the house was deserted, then I heard a scream from up here. I don't know whether it was from you or Maria. I came running up here to find you both on the floor."

A moaning from the floor near them made Vera glance around and see that the frail, dark woman was stretched out only a short distance away. She asked William Harper, "Will she be all right?"

"Yes," he said shortly, an expression of disdain on his thin face. "She'll take a while to emerge from the spell but she always comes out of it in good shape."

Vera was thinking fast now. She had no doubt that a second attempt had been made on her life. Maria could not be guilty, except as an accomplice. For Maria had been the one who'd insisted she go to the room and assist in the seance. But it was someone else who'd tried to throttle her. And that other person had been interrupted by William Harper. So all the suspicion pointed to James.

Unless William Harper had made the murder attempt and lost his nerve at the last moment for some reason. She couldn't be sure which brother was the guilty one. But now with clarity restored to her mind she knew it had to be one of them. No phantom had left those cruel red finger marks on her throat.

Struggling to her feet, she asked, "Where is your brother?"

He looked guilty. "I don't know."

In any event the question was at once answered for both of them. The thin figure of the younger brother showed itself in the doorway of the room. A look of anger crossed his face on seeing his wife apparently unconscious on the hardwood floor by the table.

Entering quickly, he demanded, "What's been going on here?"

"You tell us," William Harper said dryly.

James was on his knees by his wife examining her. He gazed up at them in ugly fashion. "She's in one of her trances."

"She was holding a seance with Miss Waters," William Harper said.

James still knelt by his wife as he asked Vera, "What went on?"

"I'm not in a position to tell you much," she advised him. "Maria brought me up here to assist her in the seance. Almost as soon as she went into her trance I was attacked by somebody. Somebody who tried to choke me to death!"

The younger man eyed her incredulously. "That's a wild story," he said. At the same time he gathered a moaning Maria up in his arms. Rising and holding his wife firmly, he told them, "I'll take her to our room."

He went out leaving William and Vera alone. She gave the senior brother a questioning glance, "Did you know he was in the house?"

"No," he said, rather uneasily.

She couldn't decide whether he was telling the truth or not. She knew they had gone downtown together to visit John Murchison at his office. She said, "You left here together, didn't you?"

"Yes." His face was blank of expression.

"But you came back alone?"

"That's right."

"Why?"

The gaunt face of William Harper took on a frown. "We had a heated discussion at your lawyer's. He wants to leave here and I think we should remain. I refused to consider a cancellation of the lease and left the office ahead of him."

"How did you get back here?"

"I wandered around in the business section for a little and then I took a taxi and came directly here."

"And James drove back?"

"He had the car."

"You didn't see the car here when you got here?"

He shrugged. "I wasn't particularly looking for it. I was still upset. It could have been parked out back. I came inside and heard the scream. You know the rest."

"I see," she said slowly. "And of course you both have keys."

"We do." He stood there staring at her. "What's behind all these questions? What are you trying to prove?"

"I want to know whether it is possible that your brother came back before you did. Apparently he could have."

William Harper's eyes took on a shrewd expression. "Are you suggesting James might have been the one who tried to throttle you?"

"I suppose so."

He hesitated. "It could have been he. But he certainly wasn't here when I came up to this room."

"Nothing to prevent his running out when he heard you downstairs and hiding somewhere until he made his appearance just now."

"I suppose it's possible he could have," William Harper said with a strange look on his angular face. "But why would my brother attempt to murder you?"

She smiled at him wanly. "You should have a better knowledge of that than I," she said. And looking at him with stern directness. "Could it be that I remind him too vividly of your niece who died so suddenly?"

He frowned again and remained silent for what seemed a long period. Then he said, "I don't consider my brother to be a madman, Miss Waters."

"You asked for a motive."

"So I did," he admitted. "I think you'd do best not to consider James a suspect. It's more likely you were attacked by some stranger. Some intruder in the house."

"How would they enter?"

William Harper looked grim. "Perhaps we'd better look into that first. Then we'll be in a better position to judge what happened."

They left the room. And Vera felt more at ease the moment she'd emerged from its morbid atmosphere. She supposed that James Harper was somewhere down the hall in one of the other bedrooms ministering to his wife. William led the way downstairs.

She followed him as he made the rounds checking on the rear and side entrances. It was not until he came to the door leading to a sunporch on the left of the house that he found one unlocked. He opened it and turned to her with a knowing look.

"There's your explanation, Miss Waters. Any intruder could have gotten into the house from the porch and left the same way."

She met his eyes. "That doesn't say that he did."

"Would you prefer to believe you were attacked by my brother or even me?" he asked quietly. "It would seem, omitting strangers, we are the only other possible suspects."

It was a challenge she wasn't prepared to meet at that particular moment. She wanted to see Henry Eden first and tell him what had taken place. She couldn't hope for a showdown on her own. So it seemed to her the most graceful way out of the situation was to pretend to accept William Harper's suggestion that an intruder had been to blame for the attack on her.

With a sigh, she said, "It could have been someone from outside. It probably was."

William Harper looked relieved as he stood by the partly opened door. "Thank you for being fair about this," he said.

"I must go now," she told him.

"Do you feel well enough to leave?" he asked solicitously.

"Yes," she said, anxious now to get away. If Henry Eden had returned she would go over and see him at once.

"I'll walk with you," the older Harper brother said.

"No need," she protested.

"I'll feel better if I do," he said firmly. And so he accompanied her back to her aunt's place. Along the way she glanced to see whether Henry Eden's car had returned and was let down to see that it hadn't. She'd have to postpone seeing him until he came over to have dinner at seven. Perhaps she could manage to get him aside and privately inform him of the murder attempt.

She wore a gray, woolen dress for dinner with a high turtle neck. It did the double job of keeping her warm on the dampish, spring night and hiding the marks on her throat. As she finished inspecting herself in her dresser mirror she realized that she had survived two murder attempts and probably would eventually be facing a third one. Would that be the decisive test?

At the moment she was convinced that James Harper was the mad murderer with his wife a possible accomplice or perhaps completely innocent. It was hard to say. She believed that William Harper's guilt consisted chiefly in protecting his younger brother whom he knew to be an insane killer. It was something she required guidance with from the retired detective, Henry Eden.

When she went downstairs she found Aunt Samantha already waiting there for her guest in her wheelchair. The old woman was wearing a rose gown that flattered her and suited her gray hair. She'd applied some makeup to her leathery, lined face and looked much less grim.

Vera touched her lips to her aunt's cheeks. "You're almost beautiful tonight, Aunt Samantha!" was her tribute.

The old woman hunched in her chair. "Not anymore I'm afraid. There was a time when I could hold my own with the best of them. But I did want to be as presentable as possible for this Mr. Henry Eden."

"He's bound to be impressed," was Vera's assurance.

And it appeared that he was. When he arrived he complimented a pleased Aunt Samantha on her dress at once. During dinner he proved himself a fine conversationalist with a host of stories about many celebrities he'd met in his career. Though he was vague in describing what he'd done for a living. But he didn't manage to fool Aunt Samantha who gave him a grim smile from her place at the head of the table.

"Come now, Mr. Eden, don't be modest," she said. "Before you retired you were a prominent private detective. Isn't that so?"

Henry Eden crimsoned. He gave Vera a swift glance and she replied with a warning look that she hadn't given his secret away. Then he smilingly turned his attention to the old lady, to ask, "Now what made you say that?"

"My Ouija board," Aunt Samantha replied promptly.

"Your Ouija board?" the stocky man sounded incredulous.

"Correct," she said. "I asked about you and it spelled out the word detective. Of course I knew you were retired but I guessed that had been your former occupation. No wonder you know the secrets of so many people. You must tell me more."

Henry Eden looked slightly embarrassed. "Your Ouija board was not completely accurate this time, madam. Though I did include some private work of that nature along with various other endeavors."

"No matter," her aunt said blithely. "I find your talk charming. I've not been entertained so well in a long time."

Even Vera felt relieved after her shattering experience of the afternoon. She'd not had a chance to talk alone with Henry Eden yet but she was patiently waiting for the opportunity. It came sooner than she expected when at nine o'clock her aunt announced that it was time for her to leave them and go upstairs.

Henry Eden was gallant and showed a great admiration for her stairway elevator. "I shall look forward to another meeting with you, Mrs. Waters," was his closing remark to her.

Aunt Samantha smiled at him. "And I shall see that it's not too long happening," she assured him. "Then you must tell me more about yourself." And with a parting smile she put the elevator into operation.

When she had reached the second landing safely they went on to the living room. At once Vera turned to the ex-detective and revealed her throat with its marks by holding away the turtle neck of her woolen dress.

"See what happened to me this afternoon!" she said.

He stared at her throat and showed consternation. "No!" he gasped.

"Yes," she said with a grim smile. "You had gone away somewhere so I couldn't let you know." And she quickly proceeded to narrate the happenings of the day.

When she finished he looked at her with troubled eyes. "It seems I must always fail you."

"I went over there knowing I was taking a chance."

He nodded. "Maria may have deliberately set the situation up for her husband. At any rate it was convenient for James Harper. And I'm inclined to agree with you. I think James is our killer."

She studied him sympathetically. "You've always been suspicious of him."

The stocky man sighed. "Yes. I think he murdered June."

"You don't think there's any chance that some stranger did enter the house by that porch entrance today?"

"Hardly. And if he had gotten in, how could he have made his escape so easily with both the Harper men in the house?"

"It doesn't seem likely," she admitted.

"Not at all."

"I had to pretend to believe the possibility," she said. "I couldn't make an accusation then and there without consulting you. It's hard to say what might have happened."

The square, tanned face of Henry Eden showed worry. "You might not have left that house alive if William Harper is involved with his brother as an accomplice in crime."

"I don't think he is. Though he may know about what James has done."

"That's possible."

"Just the same I couldn't take a chance," she agreed. "Do you think you should call in the regular police now? I could tell them my story and no doubt they would press charges against the Harpers." She was thinking of Inspector Hannigan and positive that he would act on her accusations against the brothers. Yet she was loathe to take this step until Henry Eden was agreeable to it. And so far he knew nothing about John Murchison having talked to the authorities about the initial attempt to take her life.

Henry Eden disappointed her by shaking his head. "No," he said. "I don't want to bring the police in on it yet. We haven't a solid case against them. The alibi William Harper offered with that unlocked side door would get them free of any charges."

She knew this was probably so and felt distressed. "What can we do?" she wailed.

For the first time his attitude was one of reproach. "You have been involved in this only a very short time. You lack patience. I have waited twenty years to make a perfect case against the Harpers. I can settle for nothing less."

"I'm sorry," she said, at once contrite. "I am being impatient and jumpy."

His manner immediately changed. "And you have reason. It is you I'm exposing to danger. You are my trump card in this nasty game we're having to play. If you want to step aside I have no right to blame you."

"I don't want to back out now. Not after this afternoon. I can never face anything more terrifying than the seance in that room and what followed."

Henry Eden smiled sadly. "I was almost hoping you'd ask to be allowed to leave. I've become fond of you and I'd be shattered if you came to any harm."

She smiled up into the earnest tanned face. "You mustn't worry about me," she reproved him. "I want to go through with this. I also have come to like and respect you. And I'm well aware of the great love you had for that girl whom I resemble."

There was a moment of deep empathy between them. And Henry Eden slowly drew her toward him and kissed her gently on the lips. The move came as a surprise to her but she made no protest. She recognized it as a gesture of his affection for her and as a tribute to the memory of the romance that had ended with June Amory's brutal murder. Before he let her go, the phone's ringing came as an interruption.

With a demure smile she pulled away from him to go and answer the phone. It was John Murchison on the line. With her heartbeat still rapid from the embrace of the older man she listened to the younger one who had declared his love for her only a few evenings back. Now he was saying, "This is the first chance I've had to call you and talk about this afternoon."

"Oh, yes," she said casually, keeping an eye on the living room door.

"I want to see you. I can leave here in ten minutes. Be at your place in a quarter hour."

"I don't know," she said, hesitantly.

"I'll only take yes for an answer," he said urgently. "I have some important things to discuss. Don't wait outside for me. I'll ring the bell. We can drive somewhere for a late snack and I'll tell you a few things you should know."

"All right," she sighed. "If you're certain it's that important."

"It is," he said. "And by the way, I'm still in love with you."

"I'm glad to hear it," she said, amusement in her tone. She put the phone down and went back to the living room where Henry Eden was standing before the long-ago photograph of the woman who had been murdered in the Colonial house.

He gave her a wistful smile as she joined him. "Your aunt was telling me the history of this photo. It's of the woman who was killed next door."

"Yes."

"Beautiful, wasn't she?" he studied the oval photograph again. "In most cases I've noticed that the lovely women are the ones who get themselves murdered."

"Perhaps plain faces don't give rise to such passion," was her suggestion.

He gave her a mildly surprised glance. "That's very astute of you."

With embarrassment, she told him, "I'm not going to be able to entertain you much longer. That phone call was from a friend who wants to see me. He'll be here in ten minutes or so."

The tanned, square face showed tolerant amusement. "That young lawyer fellow, Murchison, I'd be willing to bet."

She blushed. "Yes."

He touched a hand to her arm. "It's all right. Don't be embarrassed about it. I think you make a wonderful couple. And I'll leave at once. I'm not the person to intrude on a romance."

"You could wait and speak to him if you like," she said. "He wants to take me out somewhere."

"No," Henry Eden said. "I'd rather leave before he arrives. Otherwise we'll all be standing around saying polite nothings and feeling awkward."

She started to the front door with him at her side. "It wouldn't be all that bad."

"Youth deserves privacy," he insisted.

"It was wonderful having you here," she said sincerely as they came to a halt at the front door. "Aunt Samantha was charmed by you. And you must know how fond of you I've become."

He smiled happily. "Please, my dear, you're too kind to an aging man."

"I mean it. It's because of you and what you've endured, losing June the way you did, that I determined to risk whatever the Harpers might try to do to me, to help you bring the guilty one to justice."

"Don't think I'm not appreciative of that," he said in his gentle way.

"And we will win out!"

"Of course we will," he said. "And soon. I have the feeling that it will be soon." He paused awkwardly. "There is one thing. I must apologize and ask your forgiveness for kissing you when we were in the living room."

"It wasn't the sort of kiss I resented," she said, staring at him with serious eyes.

"Can you really be that considerate?"

"Yes."

"I'm disgusted with myself," he sighed. "There's nothing more hateful to me than the spectacle of some middle-aged man forcing himself on a lovely young girl."

"I knew how the kiss was intended," she

said. "And that in your mind she was uppermost in your thoughts. I understand what you've suffered."

His smile was wistful. "I should have realized you'd understand. That I could count on you for that."

"Please don't give it another thought," she said with a warm smile.

"I won't. I must get on my way." He opened the door and started out. Then hesitated, turned and said, "Good night, June."

She nodded. And it wasn't until after she'd closed the door and was standing there by herself that she realized he had made the slip of calling her by the name of the murdered girl whom she resembled. The girl he had loved. And once again she was touched. She felt sorrier for him than anyone she'd ever met. By catching the murderer of his beloved he would at least even the score, but he would never erase the brutal violence of that night from his mind.

CHAPTER TEN

She put on her raincoat and kerchief and waited in the shadowed hallway for John. While she waited she took the time to glance out the side window at the Colonial house. There were lights showing upstairs but none on the ground floor. She wondered what was going on over there. Whether or not the two brothers had settled their argument and what condition Maria was in.

More than anyone else, she wondered about James Harper. Would he be in a state of angry frustration because the attempt he'd made on her life had been interrupted by his brother's arrival? Or was his madness too deep to allow him ordinary rage. Long ago he must have been in love with June Amory and she might have been the mother of his child if she hadn't gone away for the abortion which Henry Eden suspected. Yet James had killed her and in an especially brutal manner. Her head had been literally smashed and the lovely blond hair splattered with blood and matted against her skull.

Vera shuddered at the remembered account given her by the retired private detective. Only an insane man could be guilty of such a crime. And there was a light of insanity in James Harper's eyes. All the Harpers were strange but he was the strangest of the trio. Probably he was pacing up and down in one of those upper rooms at this very moment planning the strategy of his next attempt to eliminate her. For in his madness it seemed that he couldn't allow her to live as a reminder of June Amory.

It was a shocking, sick business from beginning to end. And she was sorry that the Harpers had ever come out of the fog that afternoon not too long ago to bring this evil into her life. She glanced across the street and saw that Henry Eden's lights were already out. The stocky man had lost no time in preparing for bed. Again a feeling of sympathy for him and his plight overwhelmed her.

John drove up a few minutes later and came up to the front door. She opened it before he could ring the bell. "I'm ready," she smiled.

"Great," he said with a look of relief on his pleasant, boyish face. "I hated to ring the bell at this time of night."

"It wouldn't have mattered," she assured

him as she stepped out into the foggy night. "I don't think the fog is so thick."

"It isn't as bad as the other night," he agreed as he held the car door open for her. "And they are actually predicting a clear day for tomorrow."

"That will be a special treat," she laughed.

He got in beside her and started the motor of the car. As he turned he indicated the Colonial house with a jerk of his head. "I see some of the weird Harpers are still up," he said.

"So you now agree they are weird."

"That's what I wanted to talk to you about," he said.

"They had a fight at your office, didn't they?"

"A verbal battle," he agreed grimly. "I thought it might come to blows for a little while."

"I had some word about it from William Harper," she said.

John glanced from the wheel for a moment. "Did he tell you what went on?"

"Not all of it. I'd like to hear your version."

"Wait until we get settled somewhere," he said. "I don't want to spoil it. Why were you so unwilling to meet me tonight?"

"I had a guest. Or rather, Aunt Samantha

and I did. Henry Eden was over for dinner and the evening."

"You didn't tell me."

"I didn't think it was important. He was leaving anyway so it turned out very well."

"Nice fellow," was John's comment. "We'd be all right if we had more tenants of his type."

"And not like the Harpers?" she inquired slyly.

"That's another story," he said.

They selected the same late hour roadside restaurant and were seated at almost the exact table as on the previous night. Once again the place was empty but for a few night people and so she and John had plenty of privacy to talk freely.

He had a place beside her at the table and taking her hand in his under cover of the table cloth asked her, "What about the police?"

"Inspector Hannigan called on me. I was terrified Aunt Samantha would find out but she didn't."

"They promised to handle it discreetly," John said.

"I suppose they did."

"Did he ask you a lot of questions?"

"Quite a few."

"More important. Did he find your answers helpful?"

She smiled wryly. "I'm afraid not."

He squeezed her hand. "I don't think there's anything amusing about someone trying to kill you."

"Nor do I."

"You don't seem much worried."

"I am, but keeping a long face isn't going to help the cause any."

He considered this for a moment. "What did the inspector say when he left?"

"He promised he'd be making inquiries about the case and told me to get in touch with him if I needed him."

"Well, that's something."

"I'd say so," she agreed. She didn't want to dwell on it or push it. Not when she and Henry Eden were so close to breaking the case wide open. Changing the subject, she asked, "What about the Harpers?"

John looked at her bleakly. "I'm beginning to think you're right. They are a bad lot."

"I'm sure of it," she said.

He stared at her with fresh interest. "You sound even more convinced than when we talked before. Why?"

She knew she had played along too well. She couldn't divulge what had taken place that very afternoon without involving Henry Eden and she had promised not to do that.

So she would merely have to pretend she was taking her stand for very general reasons.

"With the Harpers next door I have more chance to study them."

"You know all about the phone calls they are supposed to have received then?"

"What James Harper told me on the phone. He was in a state."

"He was still in one when he arrived at my office," John said grimly.

"Did he tell you the nature of the calls?"

"No," the young lawyer said with a puzzled expression. "For no good reason I can imagine he shied away from the exact words of the call."

"He did the same with me. But I thought he would be more frank with you," she said.

"No. He rambled on. Said they had left Boston to escape harassment. I questioned him as to what the harassment had been about. It developed that it had to do with the murder of their niece. Of course I had already been filled in on the facts about that by the Boston bank but I had to make on it was all new to me."

"That must have taken some doing," she said.

He sighed. "I had to be careful. And all the while that James was telling me this, his brother William sat glaring at him. It was anything but an easy atmosphere."

"Then these so-called obscene calls must be linked to what he terms harassment about that long-ago murder."

"That's what I gathered," John admitted.

She gave him a meaningful look. "So you see they were more involved with the murder than you believed in the beginning."

He let go her hand as the waiter arrived with their food. "So it seems," he said glumly.

When they were alone after being served she paused over her plate of french fries and a chicken sandwich to ask him, "Tell me about the quarrel."

"It was about whether they'd stay on here or make some settlement on the lease and leave."

"William is the one who wanted to remain?"

"Yes. James Harper was all for leaving within a few days."

"That's what I understood," she agreed.

John frowned at his plate. "They bickered back and forth and I had the feeling they were hinting things at each other that I didn't understand. In the end William won out by getting up and leaving the office without any decisions about the property having been made."

"I don't suppose James was delighted."

"He nearly choked with anger," John assured her. "I think he has an almost uncontrollable temper. Yet he saw that he was balked for the time being at least. After a few minutes he got up and left. But he promised he'd be back to discuss the matter further."

"I like James the least of them all," she said, careful not to give her reasons for her feelings. It was hard to talk with John and keep so much from him. But this had to be until things were finally settled.

"I'd not given any of them much thought," John admitted. "But now I'm willing to go along with you. It would have saved a lot of trouble if I'd found someone else for the Colonial house. To put it frankly I have a nasty idea they know a lot more than they've ever admitted about that niece's murder."

"That's the whole thing."

John turned to study her worriedly. "And with you resembling the girl as you do, it could be dangerous for you."

"I wonder," she said.

"What annoys me is that I involved you. You'd never have met them if I hadn't dragged them along to your aunt's place."

"It's no use worrying about that now."

"I'm worried about you!"

"I'll manage," she said with a faint smile. "I have Inspector Hannigan to watch out for me."

John sat back from his plate with a baffled expression. "That's another thing. I can't very well go to Hannigan and suggest the Harpers may have been mixed up in a murder or tell him I wouldn't be surprised if James Harper turned out to be a psychotic. He wouldn't listen to me and he'd probably decide there was no need to watch out for you. That I was imagining the whole business."

"The best thing you can do is be patient and wait," she said.

He looked at her with puzzled eyes. "You seem much too cool about this. From the way you act I'd say you know something I don't. Do you?"

"Of course not," she said quickly.

"You don't seem alarmed enough."

"I am. But it won't do any good for me to panic."

"I guess not," John said doubtfully. "I wish the Harpers would decide to go. If they do and come to me I'll give them no trouble with the lease. I'll be happy to get rid of them."

"How will you explain it to Aunt Samantha? She's been anxious to have the house rented."

"The strange thing is she's never been enthusiastic about my renting it to the Harpers."

She smiled in bewilderment. "I didn't think of that before. She hasn't been cordial to them. She's not even wanted to entertain them. Maybe she has a sixth sense about them."

He nodded and said wryly, "Could be the Ouija board gave her a warning."

The discussion that had begun so seriously ended on this rather light note. It was time to go home. Vera felt guilty in not being able to be completely truthful with the young lawyer. She would have felt much better if she'd been able to reveal the second attempt on her life and the experiences she had with the Harpers. But because of her pact with Henry Eden she had to keep silent. It was the only way they could be sure to lure the killer into betraying himself.

John drove her home and lingered over kissing her good night. He seemed unwilling to leave her. As he was about to go he glanced at the Colonial house and said, "No lights there now."

"All the consciences are at rest," she said rather grimly.

"I wonder," John debated. "Do guilty minds get any ease in sleep? I think Shakespeare said something about it."

She smiled. "It has to do with dreams if I remember right. Bad dreams. I'm sure they must have them. And so will I if I stay here much longer talking about unpleasant things."

He took the hint and said his final good night. She went up the shadowed stairs to the bedroom which she had never been able to like but which she had come to endure. As she prepared for the night she tried to convince herself she had been right in not confiding the whole truth about the Harpers to John. But it worried her.

And her dreams reflected her worries. In them she endured the agonies of the seance once more. But this time new horror was added in that she actually saw the shadowy figure of the murdered woman moving toward her. The woman's hands gripped her throat just as she'd endured it in the other house earlier in the day. The dream followed every detail of what had taken place except that James Harper was not involved and she saw the phantoms clearly. She was slowly being strangled when the figure of Henry Eden appeared in the doorway. She cried out to him for aid but he continued to stand in the doorway seemingly frozen there by the sight of the ghosts. Now Maria rose from the floor in a badly dishevelled state and began to shriek with laughter and point a taunting finger at the stocky man.

Henry Eden didn't move but stared at the frail dark woman in horror. And next both James and William Harper came to join their sister and laugh at the retired detective derisively. Vera ran across to them and beat at them with her clenched fists and told them to stop. They only laughed harder. Then she came awake with a start.

The first thing she noticed was the sun beaming in through her window. The fog had surely vanished. At least for a day. It looked warm and pleasant outside and she forgot the nightmare which had plagued her as she quickly got out of bed to wash and dress for breakfast.

She'd barely finished the morning meal when a car drew up at the front door. It took only a glance to tell that it was Inspector Hannigan back once more. She told Mrs. Gaskell she would answer the door and let the lanky, graying police officer in herself. Again she took him directly to the study.

When they were alone behind the closed door she asked him, "Have you found out anything, Inspector?"

"We have a suspect," he said. "Just one. It's rather important that you remember that night that someone shoved you in front of the car. You didn't see who it was you say."

"No. I didn't."

He was studying her sharply. "But you did hear a footstep behind you and somebody run off after you'd been shoved."

"Yes."

"This is the tricky part," he said. "The suspect we have has a bad limp. He has a very distinctive footstep and when he runs you can tell he's crippled. His footsteps have an uneven sound."

She shook her head. "It couldn't have been he."

Inspector Hannigan's eyes narrowed. "You're sure?"

"I am. The footsteps I heard were perfectly normal."

"I see," he said with a sigh. "You're positive about that."

"Yes."

"Too bad," he said. "This fellow is the only real suspect we've been able to come up with. In the last few months he's been in trouble a couple of times. His specialty is attacking lone women and snatching purses."

"It wasn't he. I'm sure of it. I had no purse. This was a malicious attack."

"Then it narrows down to your neighbors," he said. "Do you suspect any of them?"

She knew she had to play it cool or give away the secret plan she had with Henry Eden for catching the murderer. So she said, "I've not given it enough thought."

"Would it be someone in this household? A servant perhaps?"

"I doubt it."

Inspector Hannigan's lantern jaw was set in a stern line. "There are the three members of the Harper family in the house next door. And this Henry Eden who is renting across the way. What about them?"

"My answer has to be the same. I'm not sure I could point an accusing finger at any one of them. What motive would any of them have to harm me?"

He stared at her oddly. "I thought your original impression was that you were dealing with an insane person. Mad people don't require motives."

"That's true," she was forced to admit. But with a worried smile, she said, "Surely none of those people you mentioned can be mad!"

"You might be in a better position to know that than I," he pointed out.

"I told you, Inspector," she said wearily. "I need to think about it a little longer."

He eyed her impatiently. "I must warn you there's very little else we can do unless you're able to give us some more information. I mean we need you to cooperate."

"I understand, Inspector," she said in a small voice.

He moved uneasily from one foot to the other, his eyes still fixed on her. "From the start I've felt you were holding something back. I may be wrong but that's still my hunch."

"It's not true," she said, blushing.

"I want to believe you," he said. "And I hope you're not taking chances with your life. If anything happens to you because of information withheld, I don't think you'll get much sympathy."

"I understand that," she said wearily.

He turned to leave, then paused to say over his shoulder, "You have my address and number if you need to get in touch with me?"

"Yes." And she opened the study door for him and saw him to the front door and outside. When she closed the door after him and turned she saw her Aunt Samantha coming down the stairs in her elevator.

As Vera helped her into her wheelchair the old woman asked, "Who was that tall man?"

"Just a friend of John's who came by to pay his respects," Vera was forced to lie.

"So early in the day?" the old woman lifted her eyebrows.

"He's leaving the city," she said quickly manufacturing an alibi. "It was his only chance to drop by."

"I see," the old woman in the wheelchair said. "He's handsome enough though a little old for you."

Vera forced a smile. "He's not interested in me. He made the call only out of politeness."

The hawk face of her aunt showed derision. "I've known some other politeness calls that ended with both parties marching up the aisle together."

"I don't think you need worry this time."

Aunt Samantha hunched in her chair. "What time did Henry Eden go home last night?"

"After ten."

"Now there's a remarkable man," the old woman said. "Too bad he isn't younger."

"I like him as he is," she said. "He's known a great sorrow in his life. I think he has borne up under it magnificently."

"He didn't strike me as a martyr but he is a good talker," Aunt Samantha declared. "And I enjoy a good talker."

"He's most interesting."

"Indeed," her aunt agreed. "I'm going to ask the Ouija board some more questions about him."

"Did you really find out he was a detective that way?"

Aunt Samantha chuckled. "No. I must admit I was bluffing. I heard John Murchison say he'd once been a detective. And I stored it away until I could find a proper moment to use the information. It came tonight. Very neat of me, wasn't it?"

Vera looked at her in awe. "I'm afraid you have the makings of a wicked old woman," she warned her.

"I am a wicked old woman," Aunt Samantha said with a smile. "And proud of it."

"Nonsense. You're not wicked at all. You just pretend to be."

The doorbell rang again and they exchanged glances. Then Vera went and opened the front door to have William Harper step inside. He looked more gaunt and haggard than ever and he was carrying a small suitcase in one hand.

"Please forgive this intrusion," he told

Vera and then he nodded to Aunt Samantha. "I presume you are Mrs. Waters."

"You presume right," the old woman said sharply. "And who are you?"

"William Harper."

Aunt Samantha stared at him. "You're one of the Harpers who rented the house next door."

"Yes. I am glad we're meeting at last," he said politely. Then he turned to Vera again, who in the meantime had closed the door, and said, "Though I have actually come to say I'm leaving."

"Leaving?" Vera said.

"Yes," he said, his lean face shadowing. "I'm afraid my brother and I no longer see eye to eye. It has become impossible for me to share the same house with him. I'm going to move downtown to a hotel until the matter of the lease is settled. Then I shall return to Boston."

Aunt Samantha had been taking this all in. She asked him, "You and your brother have quarreled?"

"Yes," he told her.

"That's too bad. Then you'll be giving up the house?"

"I would say so," William Harper agreed.

"Why don't you stay here as my guest

until you get this straightened out with John Murchison?" suggested the old woman in the wheelchair.

The spare, dark man looked both surprised and embarrassed. "That is too kind of you," he said.

"Not really," Aunt Samantha said. "It's possible you and your brother may yet reconcile your differences. Keeping you here may pay me well."

He looked uncertain. "I don't know whether it would be wise."

Vera wanted him to remain. Otherwise the plan Henry Eden had worked so long on might collapse. All the Harpers might move out within the day. And nothing had been proven yet.

She said, "I think you should accept my aunt's offer. You'll be most welcome here."

William Harper still hesitated. "It would be an imposition."

"We have a house full of empty rooms," Aunt Samantha said promptly. "And a cook who enjoys having strangers sample her wares."

The thin man smiled bleakly. "Thank you. Then I may accept your hospitality for a day. But just until I can talk to your lawyer, Mrs. Waters."

"Fine," the old woman said. "I'll go tell

cook the good news at once." And she began propelling her chair down the long, shadowed hall to the kitchen.

The angular face of the older Harper brother showed awe as he watched after her. He glanced at Vera again. "A most remarkable lady!"

"I think so," she agreed.

"It is very convenient for me to be here," he said. "I'll phone Mr. Murchison in a few minutes if I may."

"Of course," she said. "Until my aunt returns we may as well wait in the living room in comfort. I don't know where she wants to put you and I'd prefer her to assign you to your room."

"That will be quite satisfactory," William Harper said. He had lost nearly all his dry assurance in this unexpected predicament.

They went into the living room and she turned to him with questioning eyes. "I take it the quarrel between you and your brother is serious."

"Extremely serious," he said. And he glanced around to make sure they were alone. Then he added, "May I speak frankly to you?"

"If you like."

"I'm sure you're someone I can trust," the thin man said with a worried frown.

"After you left the house yesterday I began asking my brother some questions. He wasn't able to give me satisfactory answers to all of them. And finally I began to wonder if you hadn't been the victim of an attack by him."

She said in a low voice, "My aunt hasn't been told about it."

"Oh?" He looked surprised.

She quickly went on to explain. "I didn't want to upset her until I had more information about what happened."

"That makes sense. She is an old woman and it could unduly worry her," he agreed.

"Exactly," she said, pleased that she was handling him so easily. "And for the same reason I said nothing about it to John Murchison. I would appreciate your keeping silent on what went on at the house yesterday also."

"If you like," he said.

"Later I intend to tell them everything," she said. "When we know who was responsible for trying to throttle me. You now say you think it was James. And so have I from the first."

The thin man look distressed. "I practically accused James to his face and he went into such a fury I felt it would be unsafe for me to remain in the house with him."

"Are these rages a frequent thing with him?"

"Only recently," William Harper said. "I believe they are growing more serious as the weeks go by."

"Could he be unbalanced?"

William Harper literally wrung his hands. "That thought has tormented me for a long time. Too long a time."

"What do you mean by too long a time?" she asked at once. It struck her she might be going to get valuable information from the distraught thin man.

He swallowed hard. "You remember the murder of our niece some twenty years ago."

"You spoke of it. And of my looking a lot like her."

"You do." He hesitated.

"Please, tell me whatever you have to say before my aunt returns," she said. "We'll have to watch our conversation then."

"I understand," he said, looking strained and actually perspiring a little. "At the time June Amory was murdered James was seeing a good deal of her."

"Even though he'd recently married?"

"Yes," the thin man licked his lips uneasily. "But I have reason to believe they had a quarrel. She went away for a little.

When she returned she took me aside one day and said she had changed her mind about him. She wouldn't say why."

"You think James may have murdered her?" she asked evenly.

He nodded. "I'm very much afraid so."

CHAPTER ELEVEN

She eyed him with a feeling of revulsion. This man had been aware of James's possible guilt for twenty years and done nothing to settle the matter. How could he live with such a thing for all that time?

She said, "Why didn't you try to find out the truth before this?"

He looked down, avoiding her eyes. "I didn't dare to."

"But if you had such strong feelings that he could be guilty of June Amory's murder it was your duty to tell the authorities."

"I wasn't all that sure."

"You had serious doubts about him."

"Yes."

"Well, then?" she said.

"He is my brother," William Harper said in a despairing tone. "You must understand that means a good deal. I felt I owed him protection until I was sure beyond the shadow of any doubt."

Vera stared at the dejected man. "Surely you realized that wasn't much of a possibility without the police taking a hand in questioning him."

"Until yesterday I didn't feel positive," the older Harper brother admitted. "Not until I came home and found you as I did. It seems to me it had to be James who attempted to throttle you."

"And Maria invited me into the trap."

He raised his eyes to meet hers and there was torment in them. "I can't say about her," he admitted. "She may or may not have been an accomplice."

"And when June was murdered?"

"It was much the same. I don't know whether Maria was involved or not. But I do remember that June's attitude toward James had undergone a change. She seemed to want to avoid him whenever she could. Previously they'd been together nearly all the time."

"So that even Maria objected to their friendship."

William Harper gave her a startled look. "Yes. But how could you know that?"

"I just guessed it," she said quickly, realizing she'd almost given her position away. "I mean, it was the likely sequence of events."

He sighed. "There was a great deal of mystery about June's murder. And the situation was made more awkward by her grandmother having a dislike for James and myself."

"Why?"

"We were only half-brothers to June's father. Our own father had married twice and June's grandmother was the second wife, and her only son was June's father."

"And June's father and mother were killed in a car accident," Vera said. "I think Maria mentioned that to me." She said this to cover up for the information she'd gotten from Henry Eden.

"Yes," William Harper agreed. "A tragic accident. James had been using their car the day before it happened. Later June's grandmother almost directly accused my brother of tampering with the brakes and causing the accident."

"Do you think that possible?"

"No," he said emphatically. "But June's grandmother believed it was. She knew James and I would receive a somewhat larger share of the estate because of the deaths of June's father and mother. And she became obsessed with the notion that we might also try to bring about June's death and get all the money. To protect the girl against any danger the old woman hired a detective to guard her."

Vera was at once alerted. So the Harpers

did have some hint of there being a private detective involved in the June Amory case. Anxious to find out how much William Harper knew, she asked, "Why didn't this detective manage to save the girl's life?"

"I don't know," the older Harper brother confessed. "I have an idea he wasn't employed long. I never met him nor did any of us see him before or after June's murder. During the investigation of the crime June's grandmother claimed he was no longer in her employ."

Vera listened to all this avidly. It fitted in with what she'd heard from Henry Eden. It had been part of the plan arranged by June's grandmother to pretend that the detective was no longer working for her. At the same time she had given him a large enough trust fund to go on investigating the murder until he brought the guilty one to justice. And it seemed this might soon happen.

She said, "So you never actually talked to this detective. Perhaps if you had he might have given you some helpful clues."

"I doubt it," William Harper said bitterly. "Most private detectives are lazy fellows who do as little as they can to earn their fee. I'm sure June's grandmother was victimized by someone of that type."

Vera had to conceal the smile she wanted

to show at this comment. It was so far from the truth. She said, "So after all these years you finally are coming round to the belief that James did kill your niece. And yesterday tried to murder me because I resemble her."

He nodded solemnly. "I'm forced to believe it. And that can only indicate one thing. James is a madman."

"He must have been insane when he killed poor June Amory twenty years ago."

"I think the insanity may have been of a temporary nature then," William Harper said worriedly. "But it has been growing on him. I have seen the signs. Living with him and Maria has not been easy for me. And every time we've received those crazy calls accusing us of murder, it's gotten worse."

"So that's what is said to you when you get those obscene calls?" she said with interest.

"Yes," the thin man said brokenly.

"Why would anyone make such calls to you?"

"Crackpots!" the thin man exclaimed angrily. "There were some rotten stories about us in the press. Several reporters wrote up the trouble that had existed within our family and the shadow we were placed under by June's grandmother when the girl was murdered. To this day a lot of people think we had something to do with the murder!"

She gave him a look of quiet reminder. "It seems that James did."

At once his anger collapsed and he stood there a broken individual again. "Yes," he murmured unhappily, "so it seems."

"What do you propose to do?"

"I haven't made any actual plans," he admitted. "First, I want to get the business of the lease on the house next door settled. Then I will talk to James and accuse him directly of June Amory's murder. I will promise to stand by him if he turns himself over to the police and do all I can to get him as light a punishment as possible on the grounds of insanity."

"Do you think he'll listen to you?"

"I'll at least give him the chance," he said. "If that fails I'll go directly to the police and make my charges."

She decided that Henry Eden should be warned of the turn of events. He might not want William to take the initiative in this fashion. She must talk to the private detective before William carried through his plan. To the thin man, she said, "I think you should proceed slowly with this."

He looked surprised. "You do?"

"Yes. I'd think every angle of it over. Then act."

"You're probably right," he said.

They discussed the matter no more. At that point Aunt Samantha's wheelchair came creaking down the dark corridor from the rear of the house. The old woman propelled herself into the front hall and told William Harper she would show him up to his room. Vera waited until they had both gone to the second floor. Then she looked to see if Henry Eden's car was in the driveway. It was. And so she left the house and hurried across to see the detective.

He must have been watching her aunt's place for as soon as she reached the steps he opened the door for her to enter. She went in rather breathlessly and said, "You knew I was on my way here."

A grim smile showed on the tanned, square face. "Yes. I saw you come out of your aunt's house and cross the street. What is William Harper doing there?"

"He's going to be our guest."

"Your guest?" the detective asked incredulously.

"He had a quarrel with James and was going downtown to a hotel. My aunt invited him to stay with us for a day or two."

Surprise showed on Henry Eden's face.

"So things are starting to happen!" he said. "What brought this all about?"

"The attack on me yesterday, I'd say," she told him. "William has narrowed down the possibilities and now believes it must have been James who tried to choke me."

"I see."

"And this led him to the conclusion that it was also James who killed June Amory. He's had suspicions for years it seems."

Henry Eden looked grim. "So at last the mystery is beginning to unravel."

"Perhaps too fast," she told him. "William now wants to have a showdown with his brother right away. I tried to discourage him from that. And also did my best to make sure they all stay here a little longer."

"Good girl!" The retired detective patted her arm.

She sighed. "But it won't be long until it breaks into the open."

"I can tell that," he agreed with a worried look. "And the trouble is an accusation against James now is worth less than nothing. There is not enough evidence to link him with the crimes. We need to catch him red-handed. Then we might get a complete confession."

"How do you propose to catch him red-handed?"

"It won't be easy," he admitted. "I've had high hopes of doing so by using you as a decoy. But each time he's made a strike against you I've had the bad luck to be somewhere else."

She gave him a forlorn smile. "Perhaps next time he tries."

"I promise I'll be there," the stocky man said. "But if the brothers continue their quarrel and William makes a premature accusation of murder against James we'll never carry through my plan."

"At the best you'll have to develop something quickly," she said.

"Just keeping them on the scene will help," Henry Eden said. "Surely I haven't come all this way and gone to the trouble and expense of renting this cottage to have everything collapse."

"It will if they leave."

"I agree," he said. Frowning, he told her, "You might talk to that young lawyer friend of yours and ask him to delay the settlement of the lease as long as he can. That might serve to keep them here."

"I can try," she said.

"It will all help."

She gave him a warning look. "By the way, William knows that June's grandmother did employ a detective."

Henry Eden's mouth gaped. "Does he know that I'm the detective?"

"No, of course not," she assured him. "He hasn't ever mentioned your name. But he does know there was a detective hired to guard June for a while. He believes you were let go before the crime took place."

"That was what June's grandmother wanted them to believe."

"So your secret is safe," she said.

"For how long?" he wondered. "I must think of something and soon. This situation is developing too rapidly and in the wrong manner."

"I agree."

"I think you should drive downtown and talk with John Murchison," the stocky man said. "Make sure he keeps them here two or three more days."

"I'll do my best," she said. "Dare I mention your part in this yet?"

He frowned and hesitated. "No. I don't think this is the time. Offer it as your own idea."

"John isn't easy to deceive," she warned him.

The stocky man gave her an admiring look. "I have the greatest confidence in you, my dear. Not only do you resemble my long lost June but you have her courage."

His comparing her with the girl he loved always pleased her. She said, "Courage is not a conspicuous quality with me."

"You have enough," he assured her. Then he asked, "By the way, did I make a good impression on your aunt last night?"

"Very good."

"I'm glad. She's an odd old woman. But sharp."

"No question of that. She considers you a good talker."

His smile was bleak. "I do my best. She gave me a kind of shock when she told me I'd been a private detective. Did she really get that information from the Ouija board?"

Vera shook her head. "No. She made that up. She heard it from John Murchison."

He looked relieved. "I'm glad to hear that. For a short time I was starting to believe in ghost messages."

"She wanted to impress you."

"She did," Henry Eden said. "I enjoyed meeting her. When you return from seeing John Murchison get in touch with me."

"I will," she promised.

She left and went back to the rambling Tudor house of her aunt. Mounting the stairway, she came face to face with the old woman in her chair at the head of the steps.

Aunt Samantha wanted to know, "Where were you?"

"Over to chat with Henry Eden for a moment."

"Indeed!" The sharp old eyes fixed on her. "There seems to be a good deal of excitement here all at once."

"I just wanted to tell him we enjoyed his visit."

"Neighborly of you," Aunt Samantha commented sharply. "And what was his feeling about that?"

"He thinks you're very smart."

"Which proves he's none too clever himself," the old woman in the wheelchair said. "At least he talks well and we'll have him soon again. Perhaps before Mr. Harper leaves us. The poor man is in quite a state but I've finally got him settled in a room."

"He's weird but I'd say he means well," she said.

The leathery face of her aunt showed an amused expression. "Of course you're discussing William Harper now."

"Of course."

"I judged that."

"May I help you into the elevator chair?" Vera offered.

"Not yet," the old woman said. "I'm going to my room for a little."

"I'm taking the car downtown," Vera said. "I have a few things to buy."

Aunt Samantha raised her eyebrows. "Do be careful! The traffic is so heavy during the day."

"I will."

"And don't be late coming home, I have planned a regular gourmet dinner in honor of our guest."

"The second night in a row for you to act as hostess," she said. "I believe you're enjoying it."

"We must make William Harper feel welcome if we want him to change his mind about breaking the lease of the house next door."

"So you have a purpose in your hospitality," Vera accused her.

"Naturally!" the old woman said and then wheeled herself off down the corridor.

Vera changed to a light yellow knit dress and a matching topcoat. She considered this a smart outfit for her venture to the Portland business district. It wasn't usual for her to bother John at his office during business hours, even on the phone. But she was sure he would give her a few minutes of his time if she showed up there and asked to see him.

She hadn't yet determined what she'd

say. It was all very tricky. She had to keep in mind what she could reveal and what she couldn't. And she was glad that soon the whole business would be in the open and she wouldn't have to carry on this deceit. It bothered her to keep evading the truth with John.

As soon as she was dressed she went downstairs and out to get the car. She was on the sidewalk going around to the garage when Maria Harper appeared on the steps of the Colonial house and beckoned to her to join her.

Vera hesitated, at once feeling nervous, and called to the older woman, "I'm sorry. I'm on my way downtown. In a hurry!"

"But I must speak to you!" Maria pleaded coming down several steps.

Vera saw she was faced with an awkward situation. Taking a deep breath she proceeded to the steps of the Colonial house where Maria was standing. She saw that the frail woman, wearing one of her drab black dresses, was looking dreadfully upset.

"What is the trouble?" she asked.

Maria said, "If you'll just step inside a moment I'll tell you. I can't talk out here."

"I only have a moment or two," she warned her. And against her judgment Vera found herself stepping from the warm spring sunshine into the cold dark hallway of the haunted house.

Maria shut the door after them and then confronted her in the gloom. "I want to apologize to you for yesterday," she began.

"There's no use discussing it," she told her.

"Please!" Maria said, looking ghastly. "I blame myself for what happened. I was too eager to hold a seance. I had no idea you might be in danger."

"It's over with now," she said quietly.

Maria's dark-circled eyes were wide with terror. "You don't realize what has been going on here. William has left the house."

"I know."

"Did you know that he and James had a terrible quarrel?"

"Yes."

"And what it was about?" Maria stared at her from the shadows.

"It doesn't matter."

"Let me tell you! My husband accused William of the attack on you," the dark woman said. "And now James fears that William may have also killed June Amory."

Vera was shocked. She'd not expected anything like this. The accusations were being reversed. This was just the opposite of what she'd heard from the dejected William. Who was telling the truth? If Maria's version was correct her aunt had given shelter to a murderer. She couldn't believe that William was the killer! It had to be an attempt on Maria's part to confuse her. And she was managing very well!

She said, "I don't think William attacked me or killed your niece."

"Who then?"

"It could have been your husband."

"No, not James," Maria wailed. It was clear she wasn't sure herself.

"Where is your husband now?" Vera asked.

Maria's head was bent and she shrugged. "I don't know. He left here a little while ago and didn't say anything."

"There's nothing to be done at the moment," she said. "You'll have to be patient. This will all work out."

Maria raised tortured eyes to meet hers. "It hasn't in twenty years," she said in a tense whisper. "All the time we've lived in a world of suspicion and shadows. Each of us watching the other and wondering. Wondering who it was who struck June down that night. Knowing the guilt surely rested with one of us. We've become completely destroyed!"

Vera watched and listened to the wraithlike creature with a feeling of revulsion and horror. The skeleton hands of June and her grandmother were reaching out across the decades to touch the shoulders of the trio of Harpers and torment them with guilt. Using Henry Eden as her instrument of vengeance the grandmother of the murdered girl had managed to be ready for this moment when the murderer would surely be revealed and the other two Harpers left shattered by their silent complicity in the crime.

In a low voice, she said, "I'm sorry. I can't help you." And she quickly crossed to the door and let herself out of the house. As she closed the door behind her she heard the broken sobbing of Maria.

It was a disturbing incident. She drove downtown feeling sick. And when she presented herself in John's office she was still lost in thoughts of that frightening confrontation. She felt like someone in a daze. It took a few minutes before the sullen elderly receptionist allowed her to go in and see the young lawyer.

He got up from his desk to greet her and take her in his arms with a worried expression. "You look shattered," was his first comment. "What's happened?"

"Just about everything. The Harpers are having grand rows and each of them is accusing the other of being a murderer. I've just come from talking to Maria. She's in a state bordering on hysteria."

John looked worried. "Maybe this would be a good time to call in Inspector Hannigan."

"Not yet."

"Why?"

"I think it will be a day or two before you can expect one of them to talk," she said lamely.

He shook his head. "I must say your logic is hard to follow."

"Try and have some faith in me," she protested. "Aunt Samantha has taken William Harper in as our guest. I think he'll be our best bet. But she wants you to keep haggling about the lease if they try to make a cash settlement and leave. She wants them kept here for a few days."

"No one has talked to me today," he said. "I can try if they do come. They could just walk out and let their lawyer come to terms with me later."

"They could," she agreed, "but somehow I don't think they will. I have a feeling they've come under the spell of that old house. That evil old house! And I think the truth about the murder of their niece will be revealed before they are able to drag themselves away from it."

He eyed her skeptically. "You're taking on your Aunt Samantha's views about the supernatural. I didn't expect that."

"This is different," she said.

"I can't notice the difference."

"You will," she promised. "I won't keep you any longer. Just do what I asked. Try and delay the Harpers from leaving town."

John was staring at her and seemingly not listening. Instead he said in a thoughtful voice, "If that niece of theirs who was murdered looked like you she must have been a remarkably pretty girl." And he climaxed his statement with a kiss for her.

She drove back home feeling just a degree less troubled than when she'd driven downtown. She had no idea what might happen next. Henry Eden would no doubt try to dream up some situation to make the insane killer come into the open. The detective had been counting on using her as a decoy. Her resemblance to the murdered June was the trump card which the stocky man hoped to use to win the game. She felt strange at being treated in this puppetlike fashion and no longer had confidence that they would trap the murderer.

When she reached the dead-end street where the houses were she drove directly to Henry Eden's. He had asked that she let him know how she'd managed with John. But when she came to the cottage his car wasn't there. A surge of disappointment went through her. It was another setback.

She parked the car by her aunt's house and went inside. The big house was cloaked in silence as usual on this pleasant afternoon. She made her way upstairs to her room and stretched out on the bed for a rest before dinner.

It was dark by the time she went downstairs. And Aunt Samantha in a gown of silver gray this time was waiting for her in the living room. The old woman in the wheelchair gave her an accusing look.

"You're late!" she said.

"I took a nap and overslept."

"Mr. Harper has already come down and I've been planning to have a special wine before dinner in his honor," the old woman said. "Since you weren't here I had to give him the keys to the wine cellar and send him down to get a bottle himself."

"I'm sorry," she said.

"I could have sent Mrs. Gaskell," her aunt admitted. "But Mr. Harper showed an interest in seeing the cellar and I thought it a pleasant gesture to let him go down. It would have been nice for you to have accompanied him."

"I can join him now if you like," she offered.

"Very well," her aunt said. "It's toward the front of the house. He's using a flashlight as that part of the cellar isn't wired. You should be able to find him."

Feeling guilty because of her lateness she hurriedly made her way along the corridor and the door to the cellar which led off it. Reaching the door she found it had been left open and hesitantly made her way down the steep flight of stairs leading to the lower level. There was one dingy yellow bulb to light the way and in a moment she was on the hard, earthen floor of the basement.

The house was large and rambling so the basement covered an equally extensive area. She left the foot of the stairs and moved forward slowly into an area of graduating darkness. Finally she was groping her way along a wood-walled corridor that was almost completely black. She peered through the shadows for some sign of the flashlight's beam but there was none.

Her hand scraping the rough boards of one of the walls, she edged forward, regretting that she had so quickly embarked on the expedition. The damp staleness of the dark place assailed her nostrils and its clammy coldness made her more uneasy.

She stumbled and then something squeaked close to her feet and scurried away. She froze and let out a cry of alarm. Her instinct was to turn and run back to the stairs. But having come so far, she felt she must be nearer the wine cellar and William Harper by now. She had only heard the wine cellar described and believed it had its own wooden door. Perhaps William Harper had gone inside and closed it after him. That was why she couldn't see the beam of the flashlight.

Summoning her last remaining courage she forced herself to move on. And suddenly she came to the end of the corridor. She groped blindly in the darkness until she found a door. Then she discovered a rusty latch and lifted it open. She shoved the door inward and could smell the dusty pungency of the wine cellar. At the same time she noticed a dim glow and saw that the flashlight was on the earthen floor a distance away with its lens partly blocked by something.

A thrill of fear surged through her. Something was wrong here! She called out, "Mr. Harper! Where are you?"

Her only answer was the mocking echo of

her own voice. Her legs went weak and she was trembling now. She edged forward in the shadows toward that partially covered beam of the flashlight on the earthen floor. She'd only taken a step or two when she heard a dull moaning from the direction of the light.

She halted again and in the next instant something moved beside her in the darkness and she was roughly seized by an unseen assailant and thrown to the floor!

CHAPTER TWELVE

The shock of hitting the hard earth of the floor momentarily stunned her. Then she raised herself on an elbow to hear the scuffle of retreating footsteps. From behind her came that dull moaning once more to spur her into shakily getting to her feet in the almost complete darkness and continuing her advance to the nearly concealed flash-light.

Reaching the spot she saw why the beam of the light was almost lost. William Harper was slumped on the floor with his body masking the light. She quickly bent down and retrieved the light from under him so that she could use it for an examination. In its beam she saw the blood on the unconscious man's head and the trickle of it down his face. He was very still now and not even moaning. Sure that he was badly hurt she turned and by the bright beam of the flash-light raced back along the corridor to the stairs.

When she reached the hallway she found her aunt there in conversation with Henry

Eden. They both paused in their discussion to turn and stare at her in surprise.

Henry Eden spoke first, "What's wrong?"

"Downstairs! The wine cellar! William Harper is injured!" She gasped out the words.

Aunt Samantha sat straight up in her chair. "What happened to him?"

"I don't know!" Vera cried, on the verge of hysteria. "Someone knocked me down and when I got up I found William Harper on the floor unconscious."

Henry Eden gave her aunt a worried glance. "I'd better go down there and see what I can do. Is there another flashlight near?"

Her aunt pointed. "In the drawer of that table over there," she said. "I try to keep them all over the house in case of power failure."

The stocky man had already started for the table. A moment later he joined Vera with the extra light in his hand. "Let's go back down there," he said. "I just arrived. I came to see you a moment to hear your news. I didn't expect anything like this."

"Nor I," she said unhappily.

They made their way down the difficult and narrow stairway and along the length of the cellar. They lost no time since they had both flashlights to illuminate their way well. When they reached the wine cellar Henry Eden bent down to make a further examination of the stricken William Harper with Vera standing anxiously by.

The stocky man glanced up at her. "He's alive," he said. "But barely so. You'd better go upstairs and call the hospital. Tell them we need an ambulance here at once. An emergency."

"Very well," she said. And she left him to go back upstairs.

The next half hour passed like some kind of nightmare. Vera was kept busy and went through the motions of acting normal when she was actually in a kind of dazed stupor. She could remember Aunt Samantha's frantic questions, the startled looks on the faces of Mrs. Gaskell and the others in the house, and the ambulance clanging up to the door.

The stolid-faced attendants went to the cellar and brought William Harper up on a stretcher. The intern who had accompanied the ambulance spoke gravely of extensive head injuries and then the ambulance drove off with another loud clamor. She stood in the hallway dazed as Henry Eden came to join her.

The square-faced man was frowning. "I

checked everything down there and it's obvious that William Harper brought about his own injuries. He must have been hurrying into the wine cellar in the near darkness and before he knew it he bumped into the jagged end of a beam needing repairs. It had broken and tipped down."

She turned to him. "But there was someone else down there. He threw me to the floor."

"Are you sure?" he asked.

"Yes."

"It's strange," the stocky man observed. "If someone attacked you that certainly wasn't the case with William Harper."

"Someone did attack me."

He gave her a worried look. "Well, at least you came out of it all right." He turned to her aunt. "Are there any entrances by which an intruder could make his way into the cellar?"

"There is a rear door," Aunt Samantha said. "But I believe it is always kept locked."

"It should be checked," was Henry Eden's opinion. And he at once left them to do it. When he returned he assured them, "It hasn't been tampered with. No one came in that way."

Vera couldn't fathom it. "I still say someone seized me and threw me down."

Henry Eden stared at her. "You're certain you didn't stumble? That it wasn't your nerves that made you think the other?"

"No, it wasn't," she said sharply.

In a low voice he confided to her, "I don't want to have your aunt bring the police in yet. If you keep insisting you were attacked she most certainly will."

She swallowed her misgivings. "Very well," she murmured. "I must have gotten frightened and stumbled." But she knew this was just another lie and she hoped there was a point in telling it.

Henry Eden discussed the incident with her aunt and assured her no police assistance was required. "It was an accident, pure and simple," he declared. "We can only trust Harper didn't damage himself too badly."

Aunt Samantha brought up another neglected matter. "At least we must notify his brother and sister-in-law," she said.

Henry Eden gave Vera a significant glance. "You'd have thought they'd come over when they heard the ambulance. I suggest sending one of your maids over to advise them William Harper is in the hospital."

Aunt Samantha looked dubious. "I disagree. The word should come from one of the family here. Since it's impossible for me to go there it is Vera's duty to inform them."

She suggested, "I could phone."

"This is a serious matter," Aunt Samantha said sternly. "I say you should go over there quickly and tell them as nicely as you can. Good manners require that you at least do that."

"If you feel sure about it," Vera said uneasily and she gave Henry Eden a troubled look.

He nodded for her to agree. "I think your aunt may be right," he said. "I'm going back to the cottage and I'll be glad to accompany you to the door of the Colonial house and remain in the background until you deliver your message."

"That's most kind of you," Aunt Samantha said with admiration.

"I'm happy to be of some use in this crisis," he said.

"But surely you can return and have dinner with us," the old woman in the wheelchair said. "We have food and an extra place set for three since we expected Mr. Harper to be here as our guest."

The stocky man smiled grimly. "Very well, if you insist," he said. "I'll stand in for our good friend William Harper."

No more was said until he and Vera left the house on their way to deliver the message next door. Then Henry Eden said, "I assume you made out all right downtown. In any case this should take care of the Harpers remaining here."

"It should," she agreed listlessly. She was still in a daze. Things somehow did not seem right to her.

The stocky man linked his arm in hers and promised her, "You needn't be afraid. I'm going to remain near you. And don't go into the house."

"Very well," she said numbly. It seemed she had ceased to think.

As they reached the steps of the big white house she saw that there were lights on in several of the downstairs windows. She left Henry Eden and went up the steps and rang the bell. As she waited she looked back and saw him standing there, a comforting figure. She also noticed that the fine day had ended with the fog returning. Swirling gray patches of it were moving in now.

The door opened to reveal a grim-faced James Harper. He said, "Well?"

"Your brother was hurt in an accident at our place," she said.

"What sort of accident?" the younger brother asked harshly.

"A fall in the cellar. He has serious head injuries. They had to take him to the hospital."

"Thank you," James Harper said in an odd, cold voice.

"My aunt thought you should know," she volunteered. "We're very sorry."

"Well, now I know," he said. And he shut the door in her face.

She stood there a second and then turned and slowly descended the steps to join Henry Eden. The stocky man came forward to her.

"I take it he wasn't too thankful," Henry Eden said.

"Barely civil," she said.

"He doesn't care," Henry Eden warned her. "He's too obsessed with his insane desire to kill you. He probably thinks of nothing else."

"Don't you suppose he'll go to the hospital to see William?"

"I doubt it," Henry Eden said as they returned to her aunt's. "I'm going to have to change my plans to suit this situation. Perhaps by the time dinner is over I'll hit on something."

It wasn't until some time after dinner when Aunt Samantha left them to retire to her bedroom that he came up with an idea. As soon as he and Vera were alone, he said, "I think we can finish this tonight."

They were standing together in the shadowed hallway and from far away she could hear the distant dirge of the foghorn. Her thoughts were confused. It seemed they had been since the strange happenings in the cellar. She studied the tanned face of the stocky man with frightened eyes.

"How?" she asked tensely.

Henry Eden seemed all assurance once again. "I just checked and the Harpers are still at home. I'm going to phone them and pretend I'm from the hospital. I'll tell them William is at death's door and wants to see them. I think even James will respond to that. As soon as they leave we'll go over there."

She stared at him in bewilderment. "Why do all this?"

"I'm going to have you waiting in the murder room up there when they return," Henry Eden said. "I'll meet them at the steps of the house and somehow delay Maria. I'll pretend I'm an old friend of William's who has heard about the accident. The main thing is I'll let James go inside ahead of Maria."

"So?"

"As soon as he comes in you go to the head of the stairs and call down to him," Henry Eden said. "Call him by name. It will be like a magnet to him. He's bound to go up there after you and try to kill you. That's when I'll come on the scene with Maria and we'll have our killer!"

She shook her head. "I can't see that it will work!"

"We've got to take some desperate chance," the stocky man argued. "We have to make James attack you where I can easily step in and save you. I can't think of a better way, can you?"

"No," she confessed unhappily. "I can't seem to think anymore. Perhaps if we told John or called in the police."

"If this doesn't work I'll even agree to that," Henry Eden declared solemnly. "I've waited twenty years to settle accounts with James Harper. Don't spoil it for me."

"All right," she said reluctantly.

She waited in a miserable state while he went into the study to make the bogus call. After a short time he came back down the shadowed hall to join her with a jubilant expression on his square face.

"It worked," he declared. "They fell for it. Everything is going to turn out as I want it. I can feel it. Tonight is the night."

"What now?"

He took her by the arm, led her over to the side window and said, "We'll wait until they leave the house and drive to the hospital.

Then we'll go over there."

She looked out the window into the fog-shrouded night and saw the lights were still on next door. She said, "How do you expect to get in there after they've gone?"

He chuckled. "That will be easy. Picking locks is no problem for me. Don't think I didn't learn anything as a private detective. I have a special gift when it comes to locks."

So they waited and watched. Within a few minutes Maria and James Harper hurriedly emerged from the white house and got into their car and drove away. They hadn't even bothered to turn all the lights off inside.

"Perfect," Henry Eden gloated. "We'll be able to move around in there without causing any suspicion."

They left her aunt's place and in a few minutes Henry Eden was working on the front door lock of the white house. Vera stood close to him in a strange mood. She'd reached the point where she'd lost the continuity of it all. The wisest thing seemed to be to allow him to take the initiative and follow his orders. That was what she was doing.

"There we are," the retired detective said with satisfaction. He turned to her with a smile as he swung the door open. "Now we'll go upstairs and make you comfortable for the big scene."

As they walked up the shadowed, inner stairway together she complained, "I still don't see how this will work."

"You lack my imagination," he said. "Just depend on me."

She gave a tiny shiver. "I'm frightened," she said. "I hate that room. I don't want to stay there alone. He almost killed me there last time."

"You won't be alone in it any length of time," Henry Eden said in an almost cheery fashion. "Just now we want to get everything prepared."

They reached the landing and he led her down the hall to the murder room. The light was off in it and he switched it on and glanced around it with approval on his face.

"This will do very well," he said.

She turned to him still unable to follow his plans. "What have you in mind?"

Henry Eden's tanned face showed a knowing smile. "You'll see very soon," he promised. And from his gray jacket's side pocket he drew a pair of thin black gloves.

"What are they for?" she demanded.

"We don't want my fingerprints scattered all around," he told her. "A detective thinks of such things. I'm going to frame James Harper in such a way that it will seem all his doing. They mustn't know we jogged justice along. I don't want them to guess you and I baited the trap."

"There must be a better way!" she protested.

His glance was sharp. "There isn't! This is no time to argue!"

She backed away. Revolted by the whole business. Wishing she dare make a run for the door and get out of the house. But the stocky man was between her and the door.

He was humming lightly now and moving about taking stock of everything in the room. Almost talking to himself, he said, "We want it to seem natural and like that other time. That's important in linking crimes!"

In a taut voice, she said, "You're not just tricking James Harper into seeming to be the criminal, are you? You do know he killed June Amory."

Henry Eden was paying no attention to her. He'd moved to a side table by the bed which held a large lamp with a heavy brass base. Now he quickly removed the ornate round shade of the lamp with a gloved hand, snapped off the bulb and turning it upside down in his hand balanced it. "This will do very well," he said, as he ripped the cord from the wall socket and turned to her smiling.

"Do for what?" she gasped, drawing back.

"When Harper enters this room he'll be looking for a weapon," the detective said, holding the heavy base up in his right hand like a club. "And we'll have this all ready for him. It will do the same kind of job that heavy block of wood did on June back in that garden. Perfect!"

Terror filled her eyes. "No," she cried. "I can't go through with it!"

"You have no choice now," Henry Eden said, taking a step toward her. His eyes were bright with madness and there was a look of triumph on his broad face.

She moved away. "It's you who are mad!"

"Maybe and maybe not," Henry Eden said. "But tonight finishes something I began long ago. And James Harper will pay the bill."

"You!" she said in an awed whisper. "You were the one! You killed June Amory!"

"Yes." He said it quietly the smile never leaving his face.

"You monster!"

"She called me a lot of things like that," he said. "But it didn't do any good."

"Why? Why kill her? You loved her!"

"She turned on me," Henry Eden said, coming close to her, so that she noticed he was panting in a strange manner and saliva drooled from the corners of his thick-lipped mouth. "I was the one who made her pregnant you see. Still she didn't tell her grandmother. But when it was all over and she came back she had changed. She said she hated me and was going to tell the old woman all about me!"

"And you murdered her to silence her!"

"I had to," he said, in that weird heavy-breathing way. "I had to or I'd have lost the money from the old woman. The way I arranged it her grandmother counted on me more than anyone else. But I was always worried that the Harpers would keep digging until they found out about me!"

She was crouching against the wall now as he pressed closer to her. "You made them suspect each other! And you kept nagging them with phone calls!"

He chuckled. "Your imagination isn't so bad once it gets working. I did all those things. And when I kill you tonight and leave you here James Harper will take the blame. Not only for what happened to you but for June's murder!"

"Why?" she begged. "You're safe enough! There's no need!"

He was looking at her with torment in his glazed eyes. "I can't have you walking around to remind me! Not with her face!

You had no right to steal her face!"

"No!" she cried and dodged to the left as he brought the heavy base of the lamp swinging down toward her. It missed her head by an inch.

"You may as well make it easy for me," he gasped, swinging at her again.

Somehow she managed to avoid the second blow. Now she stumbled against the bed and was unable to retreat any farther. And the madman was lifting the lamp base for the blow that would render her unconscious and make it easy for him to splatter her head into a shapeless pulp as he had poor June Amory's.

But the blow never came. A shot rang out and Henry Eden glared at the doorway and then let the lamp drop from his hand as he himself slumped to the floor. It was John Murchison who came racing across the room to take her in his arms and support her. And Inspector Hannigan followed him to go over and bend down by the fallen Henry Eden. The inspector had his gun still in his hand.

He looked up and told them, "Just a graze. But it will take care of him until we get him out of here."

Vera clung to John, sobbing at the same time. "I thought it was all over," she cried.

"That no one knew I was here."

"Give your Aunt Samantha credit for that," John said grimly. "She was suspicious of Henry Eden from the start. And she called me tonight after she'd listened on the extension to the fake call he made to the Harpers. After that she knew he was up to something."

She looked at his stern young face through her tears. "And then you came here with the police."

"It's a good thing I didn't lose any time in deciding what to do," he said. "If we'd been a few minutes later we'd not have been able to save you."

She stared at the outstretched body of the retired detective on the floor. "I didn't guess he was mad! Not until a few minutes ago!"

"And all the time he had you telling us lies," John said.

"He was so convincing!" she wailed.

Inspector Hannigan was standing by her with a knowing look on his lantern-jawed face. "I knew from the first you were holding back on a lot of information."

John said, "Can I take her out of here now, Inspector?"

"Good idea," the inspector said. "The boys will be coming for this fellow any minute."

So John helped her out of the room which had brought her nothing but terror. She was too weak to talk and barely able to walk, even with the young lawyer's support. Slowly they made their way along the dark corridor and then down the shadowed stairs. They passed the police on their way up in the hallway. Outside in the fog-ridden night, the station wagon was waiting, its motor running and red flashing light on. A single officer on guard nodded to them.

They went along the short distance of sidewalk to her aunt's place where Mrs. Gaskell was standing by the open door with a shocked expression on her lined face.

"Are you all right, Miss Waters?" she asked, as they entered the house.

John answered for her. "Yes. She's going to be fine." And he led her into the living room where Aunt Samantha was waiting in her wheelchair.

The old woman had a triumphant expression on her lined, leathery face. "Well," she said, "so I wasn't so stupid after all!"

John helped Vera onto a divan near the old woman. He said, with a faint smile, "I don't believe she's in any condition to argue."

"He didn't harm her?" Aunt Samantha inquired with alarm in her tone.

She managed to answer for herself. "No. I'm perfectly all right beyond being frightened to death."

"That should learn you," the old woman in the wheelchair said. "Never let yourself be taken in by a man's glib tongue."

Vera said, "You always called Henry Eden a good talker."

"So he was," Samantha said. "That didn't mean that I believed all he said. Far from it. I thought there was something odd about him from the start. And when I heard from John he'd been a private detective and that the murdered girl's grandmother had hired a detective to protect her, I decided this fellow was the one."

"A long time had passed and no one else knew anything about him," Vera said. "It had to be just a lucky guess on your part."

The old woman smiled in a satisfied way. "It wasn't a lucky guess that I listened in on that phone call. That convinced me about him. Though I knew there was something bad going on from the moment William Harper was injured in the cellar."

"How?" Vera wanted to know.

"Henry Eden showed up too soon," Aunt Samantha said. "And then he was too quick to offer to check the rear cellar door and claim it was locked."

"He did rush to do that," Vera agreed.

John smiled. "It seems your aunt doesn't miss much."

"I didn't have to be smart to get on to that," the old woman sniffed indignantly. "And then he came back and said it was all right. The door was locked. And he'd probably used it to trap William Harper in the cellar and cause those head injuries."

"He must have been down there," Vera agreed. "And it was he who threw me to the floor. He made me deny that it had happened later."

John shook his head. "I wish I could control you as easily as he did."

Aunt Samantha chuckled. "He was a good talker. There's no doubt about that."

"He was a madman! A monster!" Vera corrected her, with all the horror of the nightmare in that room returning to her eyes.

"He was those things as well," the old woman agreed. "And when he saw you, it was a torture to him. It was as if June Amory had come back to haunt him."

Vera nodded thoughtfully. "It must have been like that. He kept telling me that was how it was for James Harper. And he was really telling me his own thoughts."

"The Harpers will have a surprise waiting

for them when they return," John commented dryly.

"They didn't help things with their queer actions," Aunt Samantha said. "They behaved as if they were guilty because they had guilty minds. Thinking that one of them was a killer and willing to keep silent about it. This will give them a relief they hardly deserve."

"I would say they've been punished enough," Vera said quietly.

The conversation was interrupted by the wailing siren of the police car as it quickly moved away from the house next door. The siren had the sound of a lost soul in agony, Vera thought. And surely the man they were taking away in it was just that.

Aunt Samantha sighed. "It's been too exciting a night for me. I won't even be able to spend any time with my Ouija board." And she began to propel her wheelchair out of the room. At the door she paused to turn and tell them, "By the way, don't discount the spirits too much. They did spell out that name June and nineteen forty-nine for me. I mightn't have been suspicious of Henry Eden except for that."

Vera smiled and got up and went over to kiss the old woman on the cheek. "I won't ever make fun of the Ouija board again."

"Better not," Aunt Samantha snapped.

They helped her into the elevator on the stairway and said their good nights. When they were alone she gave John Murchison a sad smile and walked over to the window.

"I can't believe it all happened," she said staring out into the fog that was even thicker than before.

John was at her side. "It might be better not to try and remember what happened."

"That's true," she agreed.

"It was a bad night for me, too," he said, touching her hair with his lips. "I thought I had lost you."

She groped for his hand and took it in her own and squeezed it. "No danger of that now. Not ever." And she continued to look out into the foggy night.

"What are you thinking about?" he asked.

"About her, June Amory," she said. "And that I have her face. It's strange to know that."

"I think she'd be pleased," he said. "To have her beauty live on in you."

"Perhaps," she said. And she knew she would always wonder about it. That sometimes in her dreams it would haunt her. The terror of the twisted lives she'd briefly had contact with. Those tragic people who had come to her out of the fog!

We hope you have enjoyed this Large Print book. Other Thorndike Press or Chivers Press Large Print books are available at your library or directly from the publishers.

For more information about current and upcoming titles, please call or write, without obligation, to:

Thorndike Press
295 Kennedy Memorial Drive
Waterville, ME 04901 USA
Tel. (800) 223-1244
Tel. (800) 223-6121

OR

Chivers Press Limited
Windsor Bridge Road
Bath BA2 3AX
England
Tel. (0225) 335336

All our Large Print titles are designed for easy reading, and all our books are made to last.